Paul Pillsbury
Memorial Book Fund

June 25, 1998

Dolphin Sky

Dolphin Sky

GINNY RORBY

G. P. Putnam's Sons   New York

G. P. Putnam's Sons, a division of The Putnam & Grosset Group,
200 Madison Avenue, New York, NY 10016.
G. P. Putnam's Sons, Reg. U.S. Pat. & Tm. Off.
Published simultaneously in Canada.
Printed in the United States of America.
Designed by Patrick Collins.
Text set in Aster.
Library of Congress Cataloging-in-Publication Data
Rorby, Ginny.   Dolphin sky / Virginia Rorby Oesterle.   p.   cm.
Summary: Twelve-year-old Buddy, whose dyslexia makes things
difficult for her both at home and at school, befriends the dolphins
that are being held captive and mistreated at a swamp farm near
her home in the Everglades.
[1. Dolphins—Fiction.   2. Animals—Treatment—Fiction.
3. Dyslexia—Fiction.   4. Everglades (Fla.)—Fiction.]   I. Title.
PZ7.02915Re   1996   [Fic]—dc20   95-14454 CIP AC
ISBN 0-399-22905-1

10 9 8 7 6 5 4 3 2 1

First Impression

Dedicated to Oscar Owre

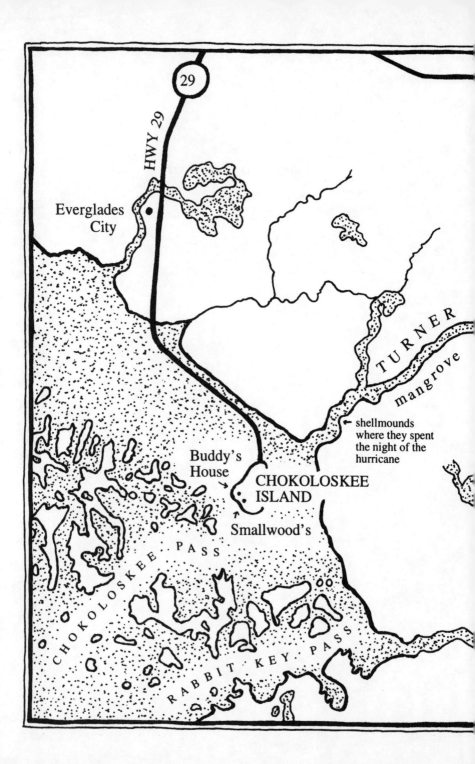

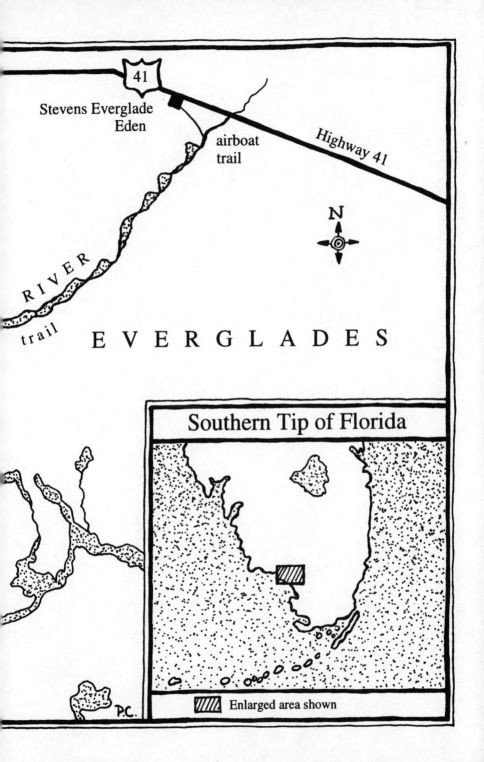

41

Stevens Everglade
Eden

airboat
trail

Highway 41

N

RIVER

trail

E V E R G L A D E S

Southern Tip of Florida

P.C.

///// Enlarged area shown

Chapter 1

September 29, 1968

IT WAS BUDDY MARTIN'S TWELFTH BIRTHDAY, and she woke up in her hot room trembling. She felt for some reason, somehow, her whole life would change today, and it scared her because she had no sense of which direction: better or worse. So she decided to believe she trembled from excitement; today a dream was coming true. Her father was taking her to see dolphins, this time close enough to touch.

The dolphins belonged to O. B. Stevens, a friend of her father's. Mr. Stevens kept them at his airboat-ride place on Highway 41 known as the Tamiami Trail because it connected Miami to Tampa, neither of which Buddy had ever seen.

~ ~ ~

Ten miles north of their island home of Chokoloskee, her father turned onto the Trail. About a mile after that a large billboard came into view, showing an airboat full of happy people whizzing past an alligator that was sunning on a mudflat. Buddy grinned. "What's the third word on that sign say?" she asked.

"Which word?" her father asked. "Famous or Eden?"

"The one after Everglades."

"Eden, Buddy," he snapped. "Eden."

"Thank you," she said. She wasn't going to let him hurt her feelings today. "What does Eden mean?"

"Paradise—a perfect place."

"Stevens Everglade Eden, five miles," she read aloud, slowly, pointing at each word. An arrow between Stevens and Everglade directed the eye to the more recent addition of "World Famous."

"World Famous," she continued. "Airboat and Pam . . . Pa."

"Swamp," Kirk Martin said. "Where do you see anything that starts with a *p?*"

She shrugged. "And Swamp Buggy Rides, 'Gator . . . um?"

"Farm."

"Farm," she said loudly, quickly, as if she had gotten it a second before he said it, "and Dolphin Show," she finished, grinned, then glanced self-consciously at her father.

He was looking at her, his dark brows pulled down.

"Longer words is easier for me to read," she said. "I . . ."

"Are easier," he corrected. "Sit back," he added. "If I have to stop quickly, you'll hit your head on the dash."

She pushed back in the seat and suddenly felt the tightness of the sandals he'd insisted she wear. She hooked the backstrap with her big toe, glanced again at her father, then slipped each sandal off, wiggled her freed toes, and turned to stare out the window.

All her life she'd seen dolphins feeding in the boat channel in front of Smallwood's, the general store in Chokoloskee, down the road from her house. But even though she'd liked watching dolphins, birds had always been her favorite animals because they could fly. Until two years ago when she discovered dolphins could fly, too.

She would have remembered that day anyway because it was only the second time her father had taken her fishing with him, except maybe times when she was too young to remember. The haul of mullet was good and so was his mood. He'd even said yes when she asked to help pull them in. And though it was hard work, she'd done it until her arms ached. And when they were done, he'd smiled and patted her shoulder as if he were pleased. Then, though he knew directions confused her, he asked her to take the wheel for their ride home.

While her father cleaned some trout that they had hauled in with the mullet, she concentrated very hard on what she would do if she saw another boat approaching or came upon someone's trapline. In her mind, she practiced right and left, starboard and port turns.

Kirk was dipping a pail over the side to wash the deck with when Buddy saw the first fin coming straight at him. She thought it was a shark and screamed a warning to him, but he was leaning over near the engine and didn't hear her.

He had warned her not to let go of the wheel for any reason. She hesitated a second before she thought to twist the wheel back and forth to rock the boat. He looked up instantly. She pointed to the two fins slicing through the water toward them.

"Dolphins," he shouted, smiled, then made a throttle-pushing motion and yelled, "give it more gas."

She was disappointed. She didn't want to get away from them, but she did as she was told and pushed the throttle forward as hard as she could.

One of the dolphins shot beneath the speeding boat. "Daddy," she screamed, squeezing her eyes shut.

"It's all right," he shouted, and made his way to her. "Go up to the bow," he said, taking the wheel. "Hurry."

Buddy stepped up on the starboard gunnel, held tight to the roof of the trunk cabin, and inched forward against the wind. When she reached the bow, she flopped down on her stomach and wrapped her fingers around the anchor rope. One fin, then another, cut through the bow wake just a foot or two from her face, like two slick, gray, finned missiles streaking along beside them. They were racing at exactly the speed of the boat, as close and as fast as if they were attached. One whizzed ahead suddenly, then dropped back into the wake.

Buddy whooped and pulled herself farther out over the water.

The dolphin on the port side dropped back for a moment, then shot into the air. Buddy threw her head back laughing and turned to see if her father had seen it. He was laughing, too, then glanced at her and grinned. And in that moment, with her father's eyes on her, warm and twinkling, Buddy felt sure she was going to cry. She turned away, so he would not see the tears if she did, and realized it was because she wished, almost more than anything, that every day with her father could be like this one instead of the way they were.

From then on, Buddy daydreamed that she was a dolphin with friends that were dolphins. They raced each other through clear, cool water, chasing boats and schools of fish, and goosing sleeping pelicans.

Chapter 2

IT WAS THE GRAVEL pelting the underside of the truck as they left the highway and turned into the parking lot that startled her back to the moment. The instant they stopped, Buddy leapt from the truck, swung at her door but missed. She left it ajar and ran toward the fence where she pressed one eye to a crack between the tall cypress boards. She could see the edge of some bleachers and a strip of brown water beyond them, but no dolphins.

Further down the length of fence, at the end of the levee that separated Stevens Everglade Eden from Turner River, she saw a plywood booth where tickets were sold for airboat rides. A large man, dressed in white, sat on a stool in front of the booth and blew on the microphone he was holding. A loud, damp whistle came from the orange speaker wired to the lamppost beside her, then the man's voice boomed across the parking lot.

"Folks," he drawled, "we got two different-length airboat rides." He hesitated, coughed a gurgly cough, and spat. "The shorter one," he continued, "is a trip that goes to the edge of the swamp and around the mudflats. That'll give y'all an idea of what airboats is built for and how they work. The grand tour is a seven-mile trip that takes thirty minutes and goes deep into the swamp to an old Indian village. There ain't no Indians living there today, but you can see how they built their village.

"We've had folks come from all over the world to take this ride," he said, smiling broadly at the few people in line to buy tickets, then beckoned to the hesitant. "While y'all is in the Everglades area, don't miss it. It will be the highlight of your Florida vacation."

Kirk had come to the fence to stand behind Buddy.

"Who's that man?" she whispered.

"That's Stevens," he said. "In the flesh. In all his flesh."

O. B. Stevens had a long torso and narrow shoulders. His arms and legs were a matched set, short and heavy, and his rear end was broad and flat. He wore white pants, a white shirt, and a red belt.

"He looks like a bowling pin," Kirk muttered.

Buddy smiled, though she didn't know what a bowling pin was.

"Orange Blossom." Kirk stuck one hand out and smacked O. B.'s shoulder, hard, with the other. "Good to see you."

O. B. snorted, spat, and took Kirk's hand.

Buddy had stepped a little behind her father when Stevens started toward them.

"You've never met my daughter," Kirk said, pulling her around.

Orange Blossom had the biggest bottom lip Buddy had

7

ever seen. And it glistened wetly. She tried not to stare at it. "Hello, Mr. Blossom," she said, putting her hand out.

He ignored it. "Call me O. B., kid. How old are you today?" he asked.

"Twelve." She smiled.

"Twelve, huh? I thought you was in the sixth grade with my nephew, Alex Townsend."

"Yes, sir, I am," she said. She put her hand behind her back and dropped her gaze from a patch of damp belly, exposed by too much strain on his buttons, to her bare toes working themselves nervously back and forth into the oystershell path. She peeked up at her father. He was looking at her feet, too, scowling. Buddy quickly slapped one foot over the other.

"She was out sick a year," Kirk said.

Buddy hadn't been sick since she was five. She glanced gratefully at her father.

Stevens was watching a couple at the ticket booth. "Well, happy birthday," he said, without looking at her.

When the couple handed the ticket girl some money, Stevens smiled, turned and squeezed Buddy's shoulder. "I'm going to make you a gift of the ticket to see the dolphins." To Kirk, he said: "Just give the girl five bucks for yourself."

"Thank you, Mister O. B.," Buddy said.

"That's nice of you, Stevens," Kirk said, "but it wouldn't be my present then."

"Suit yourself, Martin. See you inside." O. B. walked away, rocking from side to side as he went.

"Why did you call him Orange Blossom?" Buddy asked when he was gone.

"Because his initials are O. B. and someone who knows him real well once called him Orange Blossom as a joke."

"It's a funny name all right," Buddy said and laughed out loud so her father would think she understood.

Tickets for the dolphin show were sold in an open-air gift shop. Kirk bought two tickets and two Cokes. When Stevens announced the start of the dolphin show, Kirk and Buddy joined the flow of tourists through the gate in the tall-board fence and handed their tickets to a boy about fifteen who, from his shape and the size of his bottom lip, appeared to be O. B.'s son.

As soon as they were inside, Buddy darted around her father and ran toward the pool.

Once inside, Buddy could see that the "show pool" was a small, squarish, limestone pit, walled on the south and west sides by Florida holly, willows, and cattails. The east side shared a weed-choked dike with a pond. A waist-high chain-link fence ran the length of the fourth side with a gravel walkway separating it from saggy-benched bleachers.

Buddy hooked her toes into the metal triangles of the fence, stepped up and leaned out over the water. At the edge of the pool, even with the bottom of the fence, was a wooden raft with three boards missing.

To her right, at the other end of the walkway, Stevens was talking to a young woman.

"These critters ain't any business of yours, girlie," he

9

shouted suddenly. His upper lip stretched, bloodless and shiny, across the uneven surface of his teeth.

Kirk had come up behind her. Buddy stepped off the fence and stood beside her father staring at Stevens and the woman, whose back was to them.

When Stevens looked up and saw them watching, his sneer changed to a forced smile. He waved them to seats in the once bright blue "splash zone" of the bleachers, where now only the cracks, nicks, and gouged-out initials still had blue paint.

The woman held a vial of soupy water. When Stevens waved at Kirk and Buddy, she looked around. Stevens snatched the vial. He jabbed her shoulder with a round finger. "You get on out of here," he snarled. Then he dropped the glass tube onto the gravel path between them and stomped on it. He grinned at the woman, spread his short arms in welcome to his customers, and brushed past, bumping her against the fence.

She spun around. "You won't get away . . . ," she shouted, but caught herself midsentence when she saw that everyone had stopped to stare. At the ends of her rigid arms, she balled her hands into fists and glared at Stevens, then, quite suddenly, she turned away.

Because of the weeds, Buddy couldn't see the gate in the dike between the pond and the pool, but when someone opened it, the fins of three dolphins appeared and crowded through the opening. Buddy grinned to herself and watched them circle on the surface. When they arched over and disappeared, she glanced back at the woman.

Buddy thought the lady was pretty, especially her bushy dark hair. Buddy rolled a clump of her own short, limp blonde hair between her fingers.

The woman was wearing sneakers on her small, slim feet. Buddy looked down with shame at her own big feet, with their long, dusty toes and soles as tough as anchor rope. She'd always been sure that her mother had had nice small feet and that she'd inherited hers from her dad.

Buddy crossed the path and sat beside her father. "Why do you think Mr. Blossom smashed that tube?"

"I don't know. But it looked like a water sample," he said.

"Is there something wrong with the water?" Buddy asked, just as one of the dolphins surfaced near the raft. The blast of air from its blowhole drew her attention away, so she didn't see her dad shrug.

Buddy could see for herself that the water in the dolphin pool was murky and brown, like the shallow waters around Chokoloskee after a storm. She wished it was clear like the day the dolphins bow-ran her dad's boat. Here she could see them only when they surfaced, but that made watching for them more exciting, like turning the handle of a jack-in-the-box. She found herself holding her own breath between the explosions of air that announced the surfacing of one of the three dolphins.

A dolphin's gray head popped up in front of the woman who had defied Stevens's order to leave and was still at the fence railing. Buddy watched her lean forward, smile, and speak softly to it. Then there was a sudden, sharp intake of breath. "Oh no," the woman cried, leaning over the fence so far she was nearly nose to nose with the dolphin.

Buddy stood up to see if she could see what it was the woman saw. Several other people did, too.

"I thought I told you to get the hell out of here," Stevens bellowed, then glanced up at his audience. A smile cracked open around the cigar stub clenched in his teeth. "The show is about to begin, ladies and gentlemen." He flipped a switch on a phonograph and dropped the needle onto the record. A badly worn version of the Lone Ranger's theme groaned to a start. He lowered the volume and lumbered angrily down the path toward the woman.

As all eyes followed him, Buddy saw the lady, slowly, deliberately, take a small pad from the hip pocket of her khaki shorts. She patted her thick hair and pulled a pencil from behind her ear. Buddy watched her make a little drawing, write something, then jam the pad back in her hip pocket. She squared her shoulders, turned, and smiled up at Stevens whose face was inches from her own.

"My name is Jane Conroy," she said to his bottom lip. "You'll remember that, won't you?" Her smile was gone. She put her hands on her hips and stared boldly up at him. "You're breaking the law here." She kept her voice even, but her eyes were narrow, angry slits. "And it's killing these animals."

"Get out," Stevens snarled. But his bulk blocked the gravel path.

Miss Conroy, pointedly, looked both ways around him, shrugged and stepped up on the first row of bleachers.

She took a ticket stub out of her pocket, turned, held it up for him to see, then climbed past Kirk and Buddy to the very top row and sat down.

Stevens glared up at her until the record ended. The needle bumped on for a while before he finally stomped back, lifted the arm, and turned it off.

The boy who had taken their tickets came through the gate carrying a beach ball, two hula hoops, and a bucket of fish. He put them all by the fence, then dragged a folded ladder from beneath the bleachers.

The smell from the bucket spread up to the audience.

"Wow," Buddy said and pinched her nose closed.

"Looks like we got us a bad one in the bucket, boy," Stevens said to the audience. He hung the bucket on the fence and picked through the contents, chose one, and tossed it into the cattails on the opposite side of the pool. "Happens sometimes," he said and shrugged, glancing up at Jane Conroy. "Don't you folks worry none," he said to everyone in general. "My dolphins don't get no bad fish."

Jane snorted. "Those dolphins have never seen a fresh fish."

Stevens pointed his cigar at her. "I'm gonna ask you to be quiet, little lady, or I'm gonna ask you to leave."

He looked at Kirk and Buddy, then walked over, took Buddy by the chin, and rotated her head around toward Jane. "You're ruining this kid's birthday," he said, shaking his head sadly. "Sorry, kid. You get 'em like this some-times."

When Stevens's son blew a whistle, three fins surfaced,

13

came across the pool, and popped up in a row at the edge of the raft.

Stevens reached beneath the phonograph stand and brought out a microphone. "Testing," he bellowed. "Ladies and gentlemen." The microphone squealed. Stevens banged it on the fence railing. The domed top fell in the water. "Damn," he muttered, then shouted: "Ladies and gentlemen, meet Annie Tiger, Lucie Cypress, and Osceola. Take a bow, kids."

Stevens's son blew his whistle and pointed skyward. One dolphin, with a pink scar on its snout, brought itself out of the water and tail-walked backward. The other two followed. The movement of their tails made their bodies bob in a quick succession of bows.

Buddy laughed and clapped, but the silence from the woman above her made her suddenly uncomfortable. She jammed her hands under her thighs and turned to peek up at Miss Conroy, who was also sitting on her hands.

Stevens's son took three fish from the bucket he'd hung on a hook on the side of the ladder and gave one to each dolphin.

"That's it, give them their rotten little reward," Jane said softly.

Both Kirk and Buddy turned to look at her.

"Why don't you cool it, lady?" Kirk said.

Jane lifted her head and stared down her nose at him. Her cheeks looked wet.

"For their next trick," Stevens shouted, "Annie and Osceola will jump through hoops. Lucie is excused from this

14

trick because," he hesitated, grinned, and winked at the sweaty man in the third row, "because we think she might be pregnant."

The audience applauded.

Buddy glanced around at the woman. Jane's elbow was propped on a raised knee and her chin was on the heel of her hand, knuckles pressed to her lips. She closed her eyes and shook her head slowly.

From the ladder, the boy leaned out over the water holding two hula hoops and blew his whistle. For a moment the pool looked empty, then two dolphins exploded into the air.

A soft "oh" came from the audience.

One dolphin sailed through a hoop, but the boy moved the other one just as the second dolphin started through. Its weight ripped the ring of plastic out of his hand. The dolphin and the hoop disappeared into the pool.

Stevens leaned over the railing and said: "Make 'em do it again." He turned and beamed at his audience. "We'll have 'em try it again for you folks."

"It was your kid's fault," Jane called down from the top row, "not the dolphin's. You don't feed them well enough to have them do your stupid tricks twice."

Stevens pointed a broad finger at her. "You shut up," he snarled.

The boy blew his whistle and pointed to the hoop that had floated back to the surface. The dolphin with the scarred snout, the one they called Annie, brought and laid it on the raft.

"She's being awful mean to Mr. Blossom," Buddy whispered to her father, who was looking angrily up at the woman. The pleasure had gone out of this for her. She watched Annie and Osceola bounce a yellow, red, and blue striped beach ball back and forth and was glad when a weak breeze caught it in the space between them, floated it up and across the pool into a stand of cattails. Buddy didn't want them to do any more tricks.

"Ladies," Stevens hissed, making a sweeping bow in Jane's direction, "and gentlemen, Annie and Osceola have been taking dancing lessons from my boy here, Arthur Murray-Stevens, and they would like to show you folks a little of their fancy fluke work." Stevens slapped his hand over his exposed navel, and his belly bobbed as if he was having a good laugh, but his eyes were angry, blue pinpoints.

The boy blew the whistle and Stevens put the Lone Ranger music on again. The dolphins faced each other, then hoisted themselves out of the water on pumping tails. Their flippers were held up and out to each other, almost touching, so for a minute, they looked like a couple dancing, before they spun and flopped into the pool.

The bleachers creaked behind Buddy and her father. She turned to watch Miss Conroy make her way along the top row, then down the far side of the stands. Near the exit gate, she stopped and leaned over the fence. The dolphin they called Lucie Cypress rolled on her side and floated past her.

"That's it, folks," Stevens shouted, applauding loudly,

before he leaned over, whispered something to his son, then crooked a finger for Buddy to come.

She looked at her father. He nodded.

"Really?" she said, when Stevens offered to help her up the ladder.

"No problem. Happy birthday." He gave her shoulder a friendly thump, but he was watching Miss Conroy.

Stevens's son blew his whistle. It was the dolphin named Annie who swept across the pool and upended in front of the raft.

"Here give her this." Stevens's son handed Buddy a fish.

It felt mushy. Buddy sniffed it, wrinkled her nose, and turned her head. "I think this here's another bad one," she said, handed the fish back to Stevens's son and wiped her hands on the seat of her shorts.

She glanced to see if her father was watching, just in time to see the last of Stevens's customers go through the gate, then watched Stevens march toward Miss Conroy. He leaned toward her so that his cigar was an inch from the end of her nose. "Out," he bellowed, poking her shoulder, twice, hard, with his finger. "Now."

Jane knocked his hand away. "Don't touch me."

Stevens grabbed her arm, spun her and shoved her toward the gate. "And stay out of what ain't your business."

Jane whirled around. "I'm making them my business," she shouted at him.

Buddy's father was still stretched out on the bleachers, his long legs over the bench in front of him, his elbows on the one behind. "Hey," he yelled, before he jumped up and

17

ran past Buddy to land between them just as Stevens lunged at Jane.

"Get off my property," Stevens screamed. The veins in his forehead rose like buoy ropes.

Miss Conroy's back was against the cypress gate. "I'll see this show," she hissed, "and you out of business if it's the last thing I do."

"Lady," Kirk struggled to hold Stevens, "get out of here."

"I'm leaving," she said, "but I won't be far enough away to suit the two of you." She jerked the gate open with the force of a gale wind and let it bang shut behind her.

Chapter 3

BUDDY STOOD FROZEN ON THE LADDER watching the argument, wide eyed. When Jane let the gate slam, Buddy turned to see Stevens's son's reaction, but her attention was caught by the dolphins' return to their pond.

Buddy leapt from the ladder onto the path and darted out the gate to the parking lot. She raced the length of the oleander hedge that hid the pond from the cars passing on the highway or pulling into the parking lot. The hedge ended at the levee that kept Turner River from reclaiming Stevens Everglade Eden, which was really a roadside island he had created out of river bottom. She jumped a rusty chain with a No Trespassing sign dangling from one hook and ran down the levee.

The levee ended at a trash heap that spilled into Turner River. But halfway down, Buddy saw where a metal drainage pipe ran beneath the levee. It jutted out of the bank on the riverside and poked through into the dolphins' pond beneath the branches of a large sea grape tree on the other side. Buddy swung herself down on a sea grape limb and straddled the pipe.

On the far side of the pond, near the gate to the show pool, a dolphin surfaced, expelled air, then a moment later slid past the end of the pipe where she sat dangling her feet in the water.

Its snout was scraped and pink. "Hi, Annie. Remember me?"

The dolphin upended and its face cracked open in a grin.

"I came to say good-bye. I had a very nice time."

The dolphin made a whistling sound by squeezing air through its blowhole.

Buddy grinned, then pressed her lips together and blew air through them making a sound that was not at all like Annie's whistle. She laughed and shrugged.

The dolphin drew nearer. When her snout brushed Buddy's right foot, Buddy leaned over and slowly put her right hand in the water. Annie moved her head against the palm of Buddy's hand, then rolled on her side.

Buddy stroked her cheek. "You're very pretty," she said softly.

"Buddy?" Her father called.

The dolphin disappeared.

"I'm down here, Dad." She stuck her arm out through a gap in the sea grape branches and waved it back and forth.

He stepped over the chain and walked down the levee. "What are you doing?"

"I touched a dolphin." She grinned. "This is where they live." She looked up at him, her brow knotted with concern. "It's not very clean, is it?"

Her father looked at the soupy brown water and shrugged.

"Do you think that lady is right? Do you think Mr. Blossom is killing them?"

"Did they act sick to you?"

"No, I guess not. But they look kind of old to be doing tricks. The boy dolphin, Osceola, has saggy skin like the Admiral's and a white, bumpy spot by his breathing hole."

"Look, don't worry, ole Orange Blossom isn't going to let his meal tickets die." Kirk hunkered down on the levee above the drainage pipe. "I think she was just upset by the fish smell. She's probably a city gal that's never smelled dead fish without a white wine and lemon-butter sauce."

Buddy laughed. She thought about asking him what a meal ticket was but decided not to chance it. She'd ask the Admiral what that meant.

"Too bad the Admiral couldn't come with us. He'd know if they was sick," she said and was instantly sorry she had. She glanced quickly at her father. His jaws tightened, and he stood up.

"Were sick," he corrected. "Let's go."

She knew it angered her father that she bypassed him to take every question, every problem, every discovery to her grandfather. But for as long as she could remember, not one thing she did was finished off right until she told the Admiral about it. And covering her love for him was as hard as keeping her stomach from growling when she was hungry. It just rolled up and out of her.

Buddy stepped up beside her father on the levee and tried to think of something to ask him. When she couldn't, she cautiously took his hand.

A dolphin surfaced and swept the length of the pond. As it passed them it turned on its side and slowed. "Don't you think the dolphins would rather live in the ocean?"

"If they could think about it, I suppose they would."

"Should people keep things that would rather be free?"

"Animals can't want things. They aren't able to think like people do about the past or the future."

"How do you . . . How do people know that?"

"Scientists say their brains aren't big enough, or they are missing the parts that control those sort of thoughts."

"Oh." She nodded, then, just to keep the conversation going, asked: "Do you think they miss their families?"

"They can't miss things, either," he said. His voice was getting tense. "Stevens bought them; they belong to him, right or wrong."

"Where do you go to buy a dolphin?"

"Someone caught them and sold them to Stevens."

Buddy walked beside him watching for a break in the surface of the water. "Do you think it's okay to buy something that ain't selling itself?"

"Don't say ain't. It's isn't, and that question doesn't make sense. Animals are here for us to use. There's little difference between catching those dolphins to use in a show, and catching crabs and fish to sell for food. They're dumb animals."

Buddy stopped. "They're dumb?" She looked back over her shoulder. *Just like me,* she thought. *They're dumb like me.*

Her father stopped and turned. "Now what's the matter?"

"They're dumb?"

"Damn," Kirk muttered, knelt in front of her and took her by the shoulders. "It doesn't mean the same thing. It's an expression." He stood up. "Just a stupid expression."

Her father, with his head down and his hands jammed into his pockets, walked ahead to get the truck. But after Buddy stepped over the chain, she turned to stare at the murky water. She knew everyone except her grandfather thought she was dumb; she was pretty sure they were right and that he just loved her too much to believe it. But even if she was dumb like the dolphins, she was still able to miss having a mother, wish her father liked her better, pretend she had friends, and make believe she could fly.

Kirk pulled up beside her, leaned and opened her door.

If she could feel all those things, she thought as she stepped up into the truck, *couldn't they?*

Chapter 4

THE INSTANT HER FATHER stopped the truck under the strangler fig by the kitchen door, Buddy leapt out. "Admiral," she shouted, ran up his wheelchair ramp and into the house. "Admiral, where are you?" she called again.

The Admiral was not really an admiral. He was born Perry Martin, but in 1909, when Teddy Roosevelt came to Chokoloskee to tarpon fish, Perry's father was his guide and young Perry worked as mate. The president, probably because of his friendship with Admiral Peary, nicknamed eleven-year-old Perry the Admiral. The nickname stuck and now only a handful of old islanders remembered his real name.

Buddy went back to the kitchen door and pressed her forehead to the screen. "Have you seen him?" she asked her father, who was wiping dust off the truck seats with a damp rag.

Kirk jerked his head toward the shed in the backyard. "Have you looked there? He said he was going to mend my traps."

When Buddy rounded the corner of the house, she could see his wheelchair pulled up under the workbench. She bent slightly at the waist as she neared and crept toward him on bare toes.

She had never actually caught him sleeping, but she felt sure she had him this time. His white-haired head drooped so that his chin rested on his chest. His grip on the hammer in his lap had loosened, and several of the galvanized nails had slipped from his fingers and fallen between his legs. A stone-crab trap and a stack of new lath slats were on the workbench in front of him. Two mended traps were on the ground. Fifty more, in need of repair, were stacked along the back of the shed. No sound disturbed the still air except his shallow, rhythmic breathing and the hum of mosquitoes.

When she was right beside his chair, he smiled without opening his eyes. A thin, wrinkled, brown arm shot out, wrapped around her waist and pulled her into his lap. "Thought you'd caught me napping, didn't you?"

"I ain't never caught you yet, have I?" She giggled, and threw her arms around his neck.

He hugged her, kissed her cheek, then untied her arms and held her away from him so he could see her face. "Was it wonderful?"

"Oh, Admiral," she jumped up, clapping her hands together, then stopped. Her smile faded. "It was at first. I mean there was three dolphins, you could see real close and they jumped through hoops and walked on their tails." She hopped backward on her toes. "But, Admiral, there was this lady there. She was real upset with Mr.

Blossom, and he was real mad at her. They had a fight. Yes, they did," she nodded, drawing her eyebrows down into a vee.

"Really? Did old Orange Blossom punch her?" he asked, poking her in the belly with a finger.

"Nope." She giggled. "But he might have if Dad hadn't stopped him. He was sure red in the face, and all his teeth was showing."

"What was they fighting about?"

"I missed the beginning, but later she was upset 'cause she thought he was giving the dolphins rotten fish to eat. Mr. Blossom said just one fish was rotten, and he threw it away. But after the show was over they gave me a fish for one of the dolphins and that fish was rotten, too. I told Dad but he still thought the lady was just some, um . . ." Buddy looked off toward the bay trying to remember what he had called the woman when they were driving home. "Ah ha," she said, and slapped the workbench, "an overacting, good doer." She frowned. "Naw, that ain't it. I forgot what he called her, but you know what? I think Dad thought she was cute. He spent the whole ride home talking about how awful she was."

The Admiral smiled. "What did you think about her?" he asked, flattening a mosquito on her arm.

"I don't know. I think maybe she was right. Mr. Blossom's dolphins didn't look as pretty as the ones that played with Dad and me that day." Buddy snapped her fingers. "I forgot, the lady had some of the pool water in a glass tube and Mr. Blossom took it away from her and stomped on it."

"They really were fighting, weren't they?"

"Oh yeah, Admiral. He was gonna punch her."

"She kinda sounds like a nosy pain in the rear to me."

"Oh no, sir. I mean she said bad things about Mr. Blossom and talked all through the show, but she wasn't a pain."

Her father had come up behind them. "How's it going?" he said.

"I was telling the Admiral about the pretty lady at the dolphin show." Buddy grinned at him.

"Her mouth was too big to tell if she was pretty or not." Kirk looked at the two mended traps. "Did you get a late start?" he asked his father sarcastically.

Before her grandfather could answer a horn honked. "Yo, Martins." Carlisle Townsend waved to them from the stop sign at the top of the hill. He was driving his brand new 1969 Ford truck that he'd gone all the way to Miami to buy. The bed was piled high with new traps.

"Doesn't that make you sick?" the Admiral muttered, but smiled and waved.

"Yeah. The cheating bastard," Kirk said, waved and walked away.

Buddy fiddled with the barnacle scraper and kept her head down because Mr. Townsend was Alex's father. She figured he might be in the truck, too, and she wouldn't wave at him if her life depended on it. But when the Admiral elbowed her, she politely raised her hand but not her head.

Alex Townsend was always bragging about something, so it had surprised her to find out that the man who owned those wonderful dolphins was his uncle and that nobody at school had heard about them from Alex. She closed her eyes and wished the Stevens's lip on him without much hope it would work. Nothing she had wished on him ever had.

"He don't like us," she said, "why does he wave?"

"He's just rubbing that new truck in."

"I'm sorry," she said, put her arms around the Admiral's neck and kissed his cheek. "I didn't mean he doesn't like you. Everybody likes you."

He leaned back, took her face between his calloused hands and studied her eyes. "I know what you're thinking, and you're wrong. Everybody loves you."

"Just you, I think, Admiral. Just you."

"Baloney," he said, "Townsend ain't waving 'cause he likes me, he's waving 'cause he wants the oldest stone crabber on the island to see how rich he's getting. Everybody else says hi to me because I'm the most historic character around here . . .," he ran a lath slat up her ribs, ". . . that ain't dead yet."

Buddy smiled because he was trying to make her feel better, and she wanted him to think he had. She took up the barnacle scraper again and went to work scraping the slats that wouldn't need replacing, the ones the bore worms hadn't eaten.

His joking about dying didn't really bother her. Nothing she could remember loving had ever died. Her grandmother had died, but Buddy had only a vague memory of her being sick. She had forgotten crying for her. Her mother was dead, but she didn't remember her alive. All the memories she had of her mother, she had made up—one for each photograph in the shoe box on the shelf in her father's closet. She frequently stole into his room to study one picture in particular.

In that picture, her mother stood in the open door of an airplane, waving and smiling. It was a warm smile that made her dark eyes sparkle like the sunlight off the engine's prop. Her mother's long, curly blonde hair was loose over her shoulders, and she wore a corsage of white roses. Buddy could hold that picture, close her eyes, and watch the breeze move wisps of her mother's hair and see her mother's arm wave wildly with joy. And in that vision she was waving hello, not good-bye, and it was Buddy she was so happy to see.

"Admiral?" she said, brushing barnacle pieces off the workbench with a sweep of her hand. "If I'm dumb like Alex and everybody says I am, but I can still miss my mother even though I was too little to remember ever meeting her, can animals . . ."

"You ain't dumb," the Admiral said, smacking the workbench with his palm. "That sawed-off little squirt's the dumb one." He pulled her over and took the scraper from her hand. "You ain't dumb, honey. You're just like me, that's how I know you ain't dumb. You'll learn to read better. I never did 'cause of the swamp angels."

He grinned, so she did, too. Swamp angels were what the islanders called mosquitoes.

"Yep. Every time some teacher with pioneering blood

drifted down all determined to start a proper school, the swamp angels would suck'm dry and escort him back across the bay. I only know what I know because of the teachers what got here in January. The ones that came in June had mosquitoes for porters both ways. That's it by golly," he said. "You could say mosquitoes was the main hitch in my education." He grinned and held her at arm's length.

She smiled, but she was staring over his shoulder at the bay. "Is pieces of our brains missing?" she asked without looking at him.

"Where'd you get an idea like that?"

"Dad said the dolphins is dumb animals, that the pieces of their brains for remembering the past and their families, or when they was free, is missing. He said scientists found that out. I figured maybe that's why I can't read too good, 'cause a chunk or two is missing."

Her grandfather grabbed her arm. "You listen to me," he roared. "You ain't got nothing missing up here." He jabbed his own forehead. "Your pa's the one with something missing, and it's here." He struck his chest with a fist. "He's the dumb one in this family." He grabbed a slat from the table and shook it at her. "And another thing. Those dolphins ain't dumb, either. They know more about the sea and fishing than even I do. Humans is just too stupid to figure them out."

Buddy took the slat from him and laid it next to the trap. She put her arms around his neck and buried her face in its creased and wrinkled curve, closed her eyes and breathed deeply. His skin smelled of day-old sweat and Old Spice, which he used daily though he shaved only once a week. His shirt smelled of being worn often and seldom washed. She loved his smell.

He cleared his throat, gently pushed her away and tilted her head up by her chin until her eyes met his. "You ever known me to be wrong about anything?"

She shook her head.

"So there," he said. "Come on, let's head in 'fore these swamp angels drain us. Does the birthday girl want to race me or ride?"

"Ride." She laughed and pulled his chair away from the table. "Can we start from the top of the hill?"

"Sure. Where else?"

Buddy pushed him across the yard, onto the road, then turned his chair to point downhill. She wrapped her hands around the rubber grips, hooked one bare foot over a strut and pushed them off with the other. She slapped the ground twice to gain speed before folding that foot over the other strut. The Admiral gave hard turns to the wheels as they rolled down the road. "Faster, Admiral, faster," she whooped, swinging her arm in large circles like a calf roper. As they neared where the pavement ended and turned to crushed shell, Buddy leaped off, ran alongside, jumped in front of the chair and stopped it, just a couple of feet from the top of the boat ramp.

"Someday we ain't gonna make it," the Admiral panted, "and them catfish is gonna think they died and went to heaven when two big skins with plenty of meat, heads and all, roll down that ramp and land in the middle of them."

"We ain't even been gutted." She grinned, arched her back and poked her stomach out.

A sadness came to her grandfather's eyes. "At least not so them catfish could tell," he said, then looked away at the sun sinking into the bay.

Chapter 5

"I'M TAKING YOU TO SCHOOL this morning," Kirk said.

"How come?" she asked around the eggs in her mouth.

"Don't talk with your mouth full." He sat down with his plate, felt the top piece of toast with two fingers, then took the one off the bottom. "I have to go to the bank in Immokolee. I'm stopping in Everglades for a haircut on the way. You need one, too."

"I'll be late." Her first dread was school. Her second was being late for it and having to sit near the front of the class, or anywhere in front of Alex Townsend.

"You won't be late," her father said. "We'll get yours done first, then you can walk over to school."

"I don't need a haircut." She lifted her chin and shook her head so her hair fell away from her face. "It's short enough."

"Buddy, please. You'll need one by next week," he said, "and that will mean another trip for me. I'm getting everything done over there today, so I can spend the rest of the week getting the traps ready."

"The Admiral's fixing the traps," she whispered, without looking up.

Kirk snorted a laugh. "I've got three hundred traps to dip and . . . why am I explaining this to you? Why the hell are you arguing with me?"

"I hate being late for school," she answered softly.

"You hate school. You'd think the later you got there the better."

"I might have to sit near the front," she said.

"Maybe if you sat in the front, you'd learn something."

"Yes, sir." She poked her eggs. They were cold now.

Homer Dawson, the barber, had a customer when Kirk and Buddy came in, and Homer liked to chat. It was after eight when Buddy got into the chair. She gave her father such pleading looks that he asked Homer to just give her a quick trim.

Buddy came out of the barbershop at a run, headed for the seawall along Barron River. The wall was a shortcut to school, but once past the Rod and Gun Club, the backyards of every house were full of traps, ropes, and buoys. She darted through the first gap she came to, past four men dipping traps in a blend of diesel fuel and burned oil. It wasn't until she splashed through the puddle of black, oily dip that she realized her shoes were under Homer's barber chair.

She ran across the playground, climbed the railing, raced along the breezeway until she stopped herself against the wall next to her classroom. She swallowed quickly, trying to control her breathing, opened the door quietly, and slid in through the crack.

Two desks were empty: one in the middle of the first row, and the one in front of Alex Townsend, who was sitting in her favorite seat in the last row on the far side of the room. Buddy always angled that desk a little so her back was in the corner, windows on one side of her, wall on the other. Once she got positioned, she could see Barron River without even turning her head. And with the slightest breeze, she could smell its swirling blend of fresh- and saltwaters. That desk was usually safe from Alex and nearly as good as not being there at all.

Alex looked up when she came in, grinned, took his foot off the seat of the empty desk, and patted the back of it.

Buddy ducked down, crossed in front of Miss Daniels's desk, and slid into the one in the first row.

Miss Daniels looked at her and smiled. "I was just telling the class about this year's science project." She turned and pointed to the map she had pulled down from the roller over the blackboard. "Our end of Florida is unique and very important to the economy of the state. Particularly our mangroves and estuaries because that is where baby fish, shrimp, and crabs are sheltered. In other words, this area protects the health of the fishing industry, which is how most of our parents make a living.

"There is a biologist here in town right now who is connected with the Florida Department of Natural Resources. Her name is Jane Conroy, and she's here doing her Ph.D. work on stone crabs. A Ph.D. is a doctoral degree, the kind scientists and college professors have."

"Will Miss Conroy be a stone crab doctor?" Alex asked. Jason and Timmy started laughing, but Alex kept a straight face.

Miss Daniels's eyes narrowed. "Why don't you three stay after school and I'll explain it to you more thoroughly," she said. "Miss Conroy will be doing field work on stone crabs . . ."

"I ain't ever seen a stone crab in a field," Alex whispered to Jason, who giggled then slapped his hand over his mouth.

". . . instead of in a laboratory where most scientists work." Miss Daniels continued, her eyes pinned on Alex. "The project I have in mind will give you all an idea of how she goes about her study. In class, we will make a big poster, an overview of this whole area. Each of you will pick a plant or an animal you wish to study. I want you to write a report describing your subject's life cycle and where it fits in the food chain. In other words, what it eats and what eats it. You will also have to draw a picture of your subject's life cycle and attach it to the poster. Are there any questions?"

Hands waved like cattails.

"Belinda?"

"Can I do turtles? I have a pet turtle."

"You can do turtles, but you have to explain where they are born, what they eat, and what eats them. Alex?"

"Can I do stone crabs?" Alex's tone was sneering. "My father catches the most stone crabs of anybody."

36

Buddy saw Miss Daniels's jaws tighten. "Yes, you may do your report on stone crabs, but not on stone crab fishing, except to mention we eat them. I want the stone crab's life history." She sighed, then her voice softened. "Perhaps, if you see Miss Conroy around, you could ask her what she is doing for her study."

With her elbow on her desk, Buddy unfolded her fingers.

"Yes, Buddy?"

"Could I do dolphins?" she whispered.

Miss Daniels came from behind her desk and leaned over. "I couldn't hear you, honey."

"Could I do dolphins?"

"Well, sure. Do you know somebody who knows a lot about them, otherwise you would have to . . .," she hesitated, "you would have to read about them."

"Yes ma'am." Buddy knew what she meant. "Mr. Stevens is probably an expert. I could ask him."

"He's no expert," Miss Daniels said harshly. "I'm sorry." She touched Buddy's shoulder. "He's not . . . his dolphins aren't . . . never mind. He's just not a suitable source. To do dolphins, you will have to find someone else or go to the library."

Alex wanted stone crabs, the only animal anybody Buddy knew would know anything about. Maybe a bird, like an egret or a heron, she was thinking when the bell rang for lunch.

Chapter 6

AT LUNCHTIME, Buddy stood in the cafeteria line with one bare, oily, black foot covering the other. She hated recess, lunch, and fire drills, or any other time she was out of the direct sight of a teacher. She didn't need to turn around to know Alex had found her; she heard him coming.

"We need to get in here," Alex said to a little third grader. He, Jason, and Timmy stepped into the line behind Buddy. "I think Dumb Bunny, Buddy, I mean Buddy . . ." He slapped his forehead. Jason and Timmy and the third grader laughed. "I think she's changing color on us here." He pointed to her feet and the spots on her legs. "She's turning as black as a Semi-hole. Dumb Buddy, is you a Semi-hole squaw?" He cocked his head like a dog. "She ain't answering me," Alex moaned and stuck his bottom lip out.

Almost, Buddy thought, taking the next tray, a napkin, and silverware.

"Any of you guys speak Semi-hole?" Alex asked, taking

a tray and bumping Buddy's with it, nearly catching her fingers between them.

"I know a word or two," said the third grader. He raised his hand in an Indian greeting. "How cow."

Alex slapped his back and laughed. The third grader grinned and blushed.

"Maybe just moo will do," said Jason, raising his hand in the greeting.

"You're a poet and don't know it," Timmy whooped. All three boys, and the third grader, raised their hands. "Moo," they said together and laughed until they were apparently quite weak.

Buddy pushed her tray along and took what they handed her over the top of the steamy glass case.

"She don't want that," Alex said to the shower-capped server, who didn't hear him because she had never, as far as Buddy knew, ever listened to what the children said. "She wants stew—Semi-hole stew: water moccasin, gator tail, frog legs, and sawgrass stew." Jason clung to the railing for support. "And a pond apple for dessert." Alex elbowed Buddy. "Right, squaw?"

"No, no," said Timmy. "Don't you remember, she wants dolphin?"

"You want one cut in steaks or filleted?" Alex asked her, his eyes damp from laughing.

Buddy took her tray and stood looking at the messy tables and crowded benches. She didn't have anyone she always sat with, and if she took a table alone they would sit with her. Sometimes she sat with the Indians, who were always nice to her, but she decided not to give Alex the satisfaction. She weaved slowly across the room. Alex, Jason, and Timmy (they had told the third grader to get lost) were right behind her, Alex bumping her back with his tray. At the empty table next to a group of teachers, Buddy put her tray down. This was a safe zone; this was the cast-offs' table. Alex, Jason, and Timmy went to sit with some other boys by the windows across the room, and soon they were all laughing and ducking their heads to see her feet.

Buddy smiled but did not speak when Larry, then Naomi, sat down. Larry, whose mother was one of the servers, centered himself opposite her on the bench. His plate was piled high with potatoes, roast beef, and three rolls. He hung over it and jammed huge forkfuls into his mouth until his cheeks bulged like a squirrel's, then he began to chew.

Naomi, without looking at either Buddy or Larry, sat down on the bench as close to the end as she could and still have wood under her. Her eyes, tremendous behind her thick lenses, gave the appearance of being horrified by all she saw.

Buddy looked at Naomi's thick lenses and remembered when she was in the second grade her father had taken her to Doc Little to have her eyes checked.

"She still can't read," Kirk had told him.

"Do you know your alphabet?" Doc Little asked.

"Oh yes, sir." She grinned. Both her front teeth were missing.

40

"Good. See this chart? I want you to read the letters on each line as I point to them. Okay?"

Buddy looked down and flicked at his linoleum floor with her toes. "I can say the alphabet, but I don't know how to read all the letters yet."

"You know the alphabet, but you don't know the letters?" The doctor stroked his long nose then pulled down on his bottom lip.

"I just don't know which letters is the ones I know." She crossed her eyes, pulled her bottom lip out, and tried to touch the end of her nose with it.

"Look," Doc Little said finally, "the first letter is an *E*, do you see an *E* in this third line?"

"A three, a three," she hummed and let her lip go. "No, sir."

"How about the fifth line?"

"Yes, sir."

"Do you see one in this line?" He pointed to the eighth row of letters.

"Two," she laughed. She'd caught him trying to trick her. "I see two in that line."

"Her eyesight is perfect," he told Kirk, patted his shoulder and gave Buddy a lollipop. "I'm sorry, son. I don't know what it is, but it's not her eyes."

Buddy failed the third grade. Her one and only friend moved on and Alex Townsend caught up.

In the fourth grade, her father hired a high school student to tutor her. Buddy liked her, and the girl came every Friday evening for three months until she eloped

41

one weekend with a shrimper from Marco Island.

Then in the fifth grade, Buddy got Lillian Wilson for a teacher. A woman, who after one look at Buddy's handsome father, insisted Buddy's problems were "all in her darling little head." The child is just nervous reading aloud because she is shy, Miss Wilson chirped when she called Kirk and Buddy in for a conference. I was like that myself, she told him, drawing her shoulders up and cocking her head. I'll give her such special attention this year, you won't recognize her when I'm through. She beamed at Kirk, patted his arm, then Buddy's head, while fanning her bodice with a report card.

And almost daily, she was true to her word.

"Buddy Martin, will you please stand up and read now, dear?" Lillian Wilson requested, cocking her head and smiling at Buddy. "Practice makes perfect, dear," she purred. "Your father will be so proud."

"Practice makes perfect, dear," Alex Townsend had mimicked, cocking his head to one side and smiling sweetly at Timmy. "Your father will be so proud."

"Be quiet, Alex," Lillian Wilson snapped. "Stand up, dear. We are all on your side."

Buddy's shoulders had sagged at the sound of her name. She wrapped her left arm around her waist and dug her fingernails deep into her side.

Miss Wilson's tinny voice filled the still room again. "Stand up, dear."

"Stand up, dear," Alex mimicked.

Buddy closed her eyes and concentrated on the Admiral's face. Not until she could see him smiling did she move her legs, slowly, from beneath her desk and stand up.

Alex, Timmy, and Jason turned in their seats, put their chins on balled fists on their desk backs, and stared up into Buddy's face. Timmy giggled.

"Shh." Alex put a finger to his lips. "Dumb Buddy's gonna read to us."

"Start right at the top of page seventeen, dear."

"Th, Then the . . ." Her voice quivered.

"That's 'when the,' dear."

Alex patted his fingers to the yawning circle his lips formed, then began to drum the top of the desk behind his.

"When the . . . children was . . ."

Alex snorted and elbowed Jason.

"Saw, dear. Saw," said Miss Wilson, with a sigh.

Buddy cleared her throat and gripped the edge of the book as if it was the railing of a swaying tuna tower. "When the children . . . saw the little . . . g,go,god?"

Alex slapped his forehead. "Little g,g,g,god," he sneered. The children around him laughed.

"That's dog, dear. Alex turn around please. You're making the poor thing nervous."

Jason did as Alex was told and found he alone had minded. He whirled back around in his seat and resumed drumming his fingers in time with the others.

Buddy tried not to, but she looked up quickly to see if Alex had obeyed. He grinned and stuck his tongue out at her.

In a straight line off the top of Alex's head, her teacher

sat hunched low over her desk. Buddy thought she saw Miss Wilson stick her tongue out at her, too. Buddy blinked. Miss Wilson had put on lipstick and was leaning over her compact, wetting her lips with quick little licks like a snake's tongue. She glanced up and smiled at Buddy. "You're doing just fine, dear. Go ahead."

Buddy felt sick to her stomach, but she found her place and started again. "When the children . . . saw the little . . . dog and the cl,cl,clown, th, they began to . . ." Buddy stared at the next word. The drumming fingers pounded in her temples.

"Laugh, dear. Laugh," Miss Wilson squeaked.

Buddy looked up and tried to laugh. It came out as a cry, short and shrill.

The class erupted in laughter.

"Quiet," Miss Wilson shrieked. "That was very nice, dear. You may sit down. You be sure and tell your father how much better you are reading, won't you, dear?"

Buddy sank into her desk and bowed her head. "Admiral," she whispered.

Occasionally, when Buddy was called on to read, she did quite well. "Wonderful," Miss Wilson would gush, fanning her thin neck with her handkerchief. "It's night and day, the difference. Night and day. Makes all the work worthwhile, doesn't it, dear?"

However, Miss Wilson's career rewards were based on Buddy's good memory. The times she read well were when the reading assignment was given in advance and Buddy asked their neighbor, Iris Smallwood, to read it to her the night before class.

In one of her teacher's frenzies of delight, she must have tried to call Kirk only to find that they had no phone. Buddy guessed this because she saw a perfumed, pink-flower-bordered note addressed to her father from Miss Wilson. She never knew if he answered it or not, but Miss Wilson soon grew less and less interested in whether Buddy could read or not, and finally gave up. But, apparently, not before bragging of her progress to Miss Daniels, Buddy's sixth grade teacher, and suggesting that she should continue where Miss Wilson left off.

The first week of the sixth grade, Ruth Daniels called on Buddy to read. The reading was from an assignment she had given the day before. Buddy read slowly, her voice low enough that Miss Daniels twice asked her to speak up, but she read the two paragraphs with no mistakes.

The next time she was called on, it was not from an assignment. Buddy went white under her tan. Perspiration beaded on her forehead and upper lip. *I can't,* she thought, *please don't make me. I can't.* But she made it to her feet, steadying herself with one hand on the desktop. The textbook trembled, blurring the print.

Alex, Timmy, and Jason turned in their seats and propped their chins on their fists.

"Turn around," Ruth Daniels hissed, her voice low and threatening. All three boys whipped around and folded their hands on top of their books. "Are you all right?" she asked Buddy. There was concern in her voice.

Buddy nodded, then slowly began to read.

Apparently what she heard sounded perfect because Miss Daniels relaxed and sat back.

"I just read that part," Belinda Bailey said.

Buddy stopped. The perspiration on her forehead ran down the sides of her face. She let go of the desk, lifted her arm and wiped her cheek on her shoulder. The book slipped, hit the desk, and landed at her feet. Buddy stared down at it, blinking rapidly and swallowing over and over like someone trying not to gag.

Ruth Daniels stood up and came down the row of desks toward Buddy. At Alex's desk, she stopped. "I told you to turn around." She whacked the back of his head.

When she reached Buddy, she bent her face to her ear and whispered: "Are you all right?"

Buddy felt her knees buckle, but Miss Daniels caught her under her arms and walked her toward the door. Outside, Buddy stumbled to the railing and threw up.

Miss Daniels leaned against the door, her head tilted back against the little oblong window and her eyes closed. "I'd like to tie Lillian Wilson's smelly little hanky in a knot, tight around her turkey neck," she said, through clenched teeth, then, fighting back tears, she said: "I'm so sorry, honey. Please forgive me."

Whispers and giggles came from the other side of the door. Buddy watched Ruth Daniels shift her weight, slightly, and kicked the door with the heel of her shoe as hard as she could. There was a cry Buddy hoped was Alex, a scurry of feet, then scraping desks.

Ruth Daniels walked to the railing and put her hand on Buddy's shoulder. "I didn't know. You read so well the first time."

"Miss Smallwood read it to me the night before."

"You memorized it?"

"I guess so."

Miss Daniels lifted Buddy's chin and leaned down so their faces were very close. "You'll never have to stand up and read aloud again. I promise."

Buddy suddenly began to cry. Ruth Daniels turned her away from the door, wrapped her arms around Buddy's shoulders, and held her until she was quiet.

Chapter 7

BUDDY FINISHED HER LUNCH with Larry and Naomi but not
without thinking about the second most hated part of her
school day. Gym class. For Buddy it was a time set aside
each day for children to ridicule one another. At least the
school's coach, Mr. Johnson, sent the boys to the far side
of the playground once he'd chosen that day's team captains. His selection was meant to give everyone a chance
at the job, but even he had never picked Buddy, Naomi, or
Larry for the boys' team.

Every day it was the same, after the captains for the
teams were selected, the rest of them formed a line. Today
it was softball. Buddy stood a little apart from the others,
her trap-dip-covered toes rooting into the sand of the dia-
mond. Either she or Naomi would be the last chosen.

A Great Blue heron was fishing on the far bank of the
river. When the teams were chosen, Buddy took the seat
at the very end of the bench where she could watch
him.

She was still watching him when someone punched her. She looked up to see that the girl who had been sitting next to her on the bench was standing at home base holding the bat out to her. Buddy rarely batted, and the few times she had she'd always struck out. She stood up, amid moans and groans, and walked slowly to the plate. When she reached to take the bat, the girl dropped it. "There's the bat, dummy, try not to hit yourself in the head with it."

Buddy picked it up and held it out like everyone else did, but she didn't swing at the pitches. The first pitch was a ball. Someone clapped but was silenced by a teammate. Buddy looked across at the heron. The second pitch was a strike.

"You just gonna stand there?" someone yelled.

Buddy swung low at the next one.

"That was a ball, you idiot," cried the captain. "Here comes out three," she muttered to the others.

Buddy wanted to sit down. She felt dizzy and swayed slightly. A ball whizzed past her head.

"Ball two," the umpire called.

Out of the corner of her eye, she saw the heron stab a fish and step up on the bank.

The pitcher wound up and threw again.

"Swing," someone screamed.

Buddy closed her eyes and swung as hard as she could. The crack of the bat stung her hands. She dropped it in the dirt.

"Run," the girls screamed. "Run, dummy, it's a homer."

Buddy looked at them, then whirled and ran toward the base. The rush of air against her damp skin was cool; the hair on her arms prickled as it dried. She could hear the children shouting, screaming her name. She slapped past the first base and raced toward second. She was running faster than she had ever run. She grinned as she rounded second and swept toward third. Her eyes followed the heron as it flew up river. Buddy felt as if she, too, had taken flight, had lifted off, leaving the playground far below. The screams of the children faded until she could no longer hear them at all. No one could reach her. No one did. Home plate grew larger and larger. Chill bumps spread down her arms and legs. She slid into the flat little sandbag like she'd seen the boys do. Then she put her head back and laughed.

Sets of brown legs covered with fuzzy blonde hair gathered around her. She was grinning when she looked up into their quiet, sneering faces.

"You're so stupid," said one of the girls. They turned, all the little girls, and scattered to their positions on the field.

Buddy watched their backs as the incoming team filed past her, snickering, thanking her. One of the girls was carrying the ball, retrieved from the yard of a nearby house. When she passed Buddy, she tapped her shoulder. "You're out," she said, and her teammates laughed.

"You ran like a deer," Coach Johnson said. His hand was out to help her up, but she was too confused to take it. "But you ran the wrong way." He patted her back. "Maybe next time."

Buddy sat by the sandbag and looked left, toward

where the sun rises, the direction she had run. She looked to the right, toward the river where the heron had been.

"You gonna sit there all day?" the catcher asked, smacking the ball into her glove.

Buddy didn't look at her or answer. She got up, walked straight out from home plate, past the pitcher, past second base, into the outfield, out of the school yard, down the road to the traffic circle. At the bridge on Highway 29, she started to run, and she ran until she was running as fast as she had run the bases. Then she pushed harder, ran faster, her arms pumping at her sides, and the wind in her face drying her cheeks. And she didn't stop running until she had crossed the bridge, until she was on the island, home and safe.

She heard hammering coming from the shed as she came over the hill above their house. She stopped to catch her breath, then pulled the hem of her shirt out of her shorts and wiped the sweat from her face and neck before crossing the yard.

"Hi, Admiral." She kissed his cheek.

"Hi, yourself. You're early, ain't you?"

"A little."

"How was school?" He looked up into her face.

"The same." She turned and took the scraper from a nail on the wall and started working on the back side of the trap.

"I didn't hear the bus." He was watching her.

"I missed it." She didn't look at him.

He reached and took the scraper out of her hand. "Come with me," he said.

"Oh, Admiral," she cried as they came around the side of the shed. "For me?"

"Got your name on it, don't it?"

Resting on two wheelchair-height sawhorses, in the shade of an avocado tree, was the Admiral's old pitpan from his alligator hunting days. It was a short, wooden rectangle of a boat, small enough to be carried on a man's back when the water got so shallow he had to wade between gator holes. Its bottom glistened with wet red paint, and he had painted BUDDY'S on the stern in tall black letters.

She threw her arms around his neck. "Thank you, thank you," she cried, then danced around it, twirled, and stopped in front of him. "It's beautiful."

"I've gotta add a couple oarlocks and patch a plank or two, otherwise, she seems seaworthy. We'll test her," he said and grinned, "then I'll show you the way up to see them dolphins of yours again."

"Oh, Admiral," she clapped her hands together, then dropped her arms to her sides. "Are you teasing me?"

" 'Course I ain't teasing you."

"How?"

"Up Turner River." He tested the paint with his finger.

"Dad'll never let us go."

"I'll handle him. You just follow my lead." He grinned. "What's all over your feet?"

"Trap dip."

"Well good. That's good." He laughed. "It'll keep the bore worms out of your toes."

Chapter 8

"WELL," SAID THE ADMIRAL, that same night at dinner. "So you said them dolphins is in a pen up on Tamiami Trail, huh? Must be right near Turner River." He accepted the platter of broiled yellowtail.

Buddy grinned at her grandfather. "Yes, sir," she said. "The airboat rides is along the river."

The Admiral glanced at Kirk then winked at her. "You know," he said, "Turner River comes into the bay just north of here. The Calusas, and later the Seminoles, used it like a highway from their camps. Heck, wasn't that long ago, I knew that river like the back of my hand. Used it to get up into the 'glades to hunt. Good fishing in that river," he said, chewing a piece of fish thoughtfully. "I 'spect the river's overgrown in places, but I betcha we could find the way."

Buddy felt she was about to laugh. She ducked her head low over her plate but took her cue. "Up the river?"

"Sure."

"To see the dolphins again?"

"Yep."

"Don't be ridiculous," Kirk said.

Buddy watched her grandfather.

His eyes narrowed. "Yep," he said, "it's been too long since I've been up that river." He looked at her and grinned. "I was thinking maybe you and me could clean up the old pitpan and give it a try."

Buddy glanced quickly at her father, who had gotten up for a beer and was standing at the sink looking out the window at the docks. "Could we?" she asked him.

"No, you couldn't," Kirk said, turning. "What the hell are you talking about, you old fool?" He moved to the end of the table opposite his father, leaned on one fist, and shook his beer bottle at him. "You're going to patch the pitpan? I can't even get you to stay awake and patch crab traps."

"We'll do the traps before we go," Buddy whispered.

"We?" Kirk looked at her, and gave a short laugh.

She sagged in her chair like an leaky inner tube.

Kirk leaned forward toward his father. "On your little cruise, where are you going to put your wheelchair? On skis, maybe?"

The Admiral smacked the table with the palm of his hand. "It will fit between the blocks I put in," he hissed.

"You've put blocks in? You've already put blocks in? You two have this all planned, don't you?" He slammed the empty beer bottle down on the table and leaned toward Buddy. "You're not going," he shouted.

"Aye, aye, Captain," the Admiral snapped, and saluted his son.

Guilt swept over Buddy. It seemed every argument was because of her. She slid out of her chair, stopped at the door to the living room and looked back at her grandfather. He was watching Kirk who stomped to the refrigerator, grabbed another beer and went out the back door, letting it bang shut behind him.

Buddy crossed the living room and slipped out onto the front porch. Her father was standing on the seawall with his back to the house. She tiptoed to the far side of the porch, ducked under the railing and padded away into the darkness.

Smallwood's store was a red, tin-roofed, rambling, hard-pine building anchored atop eight-foot pilings. In the dark, it looked like a giant, black, rectangular spider, but Buddy still liked it best at night. She would go there just to sit on the seawall under the store and watch the foamy white lip of the bay seep in and out of the rusty pile of engines dumped there during World War II, to keep the government from making bullets out of them. When a boat passed in the channel, the waves its wake created caused the motors to make little sucking sounds, hiss and occasionally sigh, as if life was being breathed back into them.

She loved the engines. They had faces, cracked and old like the Admiral's. She put her toes in with them so she could watch and feel the water rise and fall as rhythmically as the Admiral's chest when he was sleeping.

Nowadays she found it hard to recall that she had once been afraid of the store. She was six when the Admiral told her the story of "Bloody" Ed Watson, who had lived on Chatham River, down the coast from Chokoloskee. He grew sugarcane and made syrup to sell to moonshiners for what people called "low-bush lightning," a blend of cane syrup and Red Devil lye for moonshine so strong it lathered like soap.

At cane-cutting time, the Admiral told her, Watson would go to Naples and hire folks with no kin. When the crop was in, instead of paying them, he shot them and buried them around his farm.

For a couple of years Buddy had a recurring nightmare in which her father took her to Watson's farm and gave her to him. "She's worthless to me," he told Watson. "Maybe you can get some work out of her."

After the cane was cut and boiled and the syrup was put in tins, Watson chased her with his shotgun, shouting, "Come back, I want to pay you."

She always ran away from him down the bank of the Chatham River. And each time, at the same spot, she turned to see Watson taking aim and tripped over the rotten remains of three-hundred-pound Hannah Smith's leg sticking out of the mudbank. She'd fall, hear the crack of the shotgun blast, and wake up.

It was after clam diggers found Hannah Smith's body that the men of Chokoloskee killed Ed Watson. "Killed him right there on Smallwood's dock," the Admiral said. "Right where them rusty engines is now." And after they killed him, they found fifty bodies buried on his farm, he told her. "'Course no telling if that was all of them."

Sometime, a few years later, her grandfather found out she was afraid of the store, and he must have realized that he had frightened her with that story because one evening, just before his accident, he walked there with her and they sat on the seawall and watched dolphins fishing in the channel. He told her about Teddy Roosevelt and the Calusa Indians and the history of the shellmounds. After that, the store became theirs and she went there often, though now she went alone.

Chapter 9

THE SATURDAY FOLLOWING the day the Admiral had surprised her with the pitpan, Buddy tapped softly on his door before opening it a crack to peek in. He was in his chair, waiting. He smiled when he saw her, pressed a crooked finger to his lips and winked. One hand was behind his back. "I got something for you," he said, grinning toothlessly, and pulled out a red plaid hunting cap. He smacked it against his knee, waved away the eruption of dust, then held it out to her.

"Oh, Admiral."

"It's old," he said, holding it out to her with both hands, "but it ain't never been wore. I bought it for your pa twenty-five years ago. He didn't want it. Said it was a redneck's cap." Her grandfather scratched at something on the brim then lifted it to her again. "It'll keep the spiders out of your hair when we go through where the mangroves is thick and low."

When she leaned over, he pushed her bangs off her

forehead and fitted the cap snugly on her head. She stood up, looked at herself in the mirror and smiled. "I've been wanting one of these." She turned sideways, pulled the bill a little lower over her eyes and grinned. "I love it. Oh, yes, sir," she said, placing her palms flat on his dresser and lifting her chin to the mirror. "I really been needing one just like this." She leaned toward her image in the cloudy mirror. "Admiral, you know something? When I'm looking in a mirror is the only time everything's where it's suppose to be."

"Yeah, I know. It's that way for me, too."

She came back and squeezed into the chair beside him, pushed the cap back on her head, and put her head on his shoulder. "I'm glad Daddy didn't want it."

"He was just young and full of beans when he slung that cap back at me. It hurt then, but I don't blame him now. He didn't want to spend his life hauling nets and traps like his pa."

Buddy turned the cap around so the bill was in the back. "Admiral," she said, tracing the path of a blue vein in the top of his hand, "if he hates fishing, why's he doing it?"

" 'Cause he found out he hated the rat race in Miami more. And after your ma died, he needed help taking care of you. You was such a little thing then."

Buddy took his hand and gathered his gnarled fingers into a pack, one at a time. She held them in her fist and looked up at him. "Admiral." She let his fingers go. "Why has Daddy always called me Buddy instead of my name?"

Her grandfather stared up at the large stain on the ceiling where the roof had leaked during the hurricane of '48. "I 'spect 'cause Elizabeth was such a big name for a little girl," he said.

"It was Momma's name, too, wasn't it?"

"Yes. But I don't think that's the reason. Your pa just didn't know much about being a father. He called you his little buddy from the day you came here. I 'spect he was planning on you two being pals."

"We ain't though. He's cross with me all the time."

"He works hard, honey. Especially now with me in this thing. One day when he's not bone-tired, he'll figure out what a prize he's got in you. I know that for sure." He caught her chin and tilted her head up. "You believe the Admiral, don't you?"

"Yes, sir." She took the cap off and rubbed the material between her fingers. "You think we should invite him to go with us up the river?"

"That's nice, sweetie, but he ain't even gonna like *us* going. I picked today 'cause he's busy getting the last of his traps weighted with concrete, too busy to fuss with us."

"Did you tell him we was going today?"

"I wasn't planning to, but I guess I need him to put me and this damn thing . . . ," he smacked the armrest of his wheelchair, ". . . in the boat." He grinned suddenly. "This sure is gonna make him mad."

When Kirk called them for breakfast, Buddy went to get the Admiral and pushed him to the kitchen door. He put a finger to his lips. "Wait here a minute," he whispered, butted the door open with his knees and wheeled across the pitted linoleum to his spot at the table. "I'm taking Buddy up the river today," she heard him say. She pushed the door open enough to see through the crack.

Kirk had a loaf of bread in his hand when he turned. He put the end of the wrapper in his mouth, sucked the air out, spun and knotted it. "Which river, you crazy old coot, the Chattahoochee?"

"Turner."

"Yeah? That's nice." He added a dash of Tabasco to the eggs he was stirring. "In the pitpan, huh?"

"Yep."

"You are nuts," Kirk said, not cruelly or crossly, but with a hint of admiration. He scraped the eggs onto three plates, felt the toast, muttered to himself, and put two slices on each plate. On his way to the table, he kicked open the swinging door. "Buddy. Breakfast."

Buddy plastered herself against the wall.

"Buddy, now," her father shouted. "Your eggs are getting cold."

"Like the toast," the Admiral called.

"Anytime you want to take over the cooking and give up riverboat piloting, be my guest."

Buddy ran on tiptoes to her bedroom, grabbed her cap off the bedpost, and dashed to the kitchen door. She took a deep breath, put her cap on and went in. "Hi, Daddy."

Kirk only nodded, his mouth full.

She grinned at her grandfather, and turned her head first one way then the other, so he could see the fishing

61

lures she had attached to her cap. Then she turned all the way around in her chair, so he could see where she had carefully printed her name on the back with a laundry marker: BUDDY.

"That's a good-looking cap you got there. Don't you think so?" he said to Kirk.

"Yeah." He scooped up a forkful of eggs, brought it to his mouth, and stopped. "You really think you're going to do this, don't you, you old fool?"

"Watch who you're calling old or a fool," the Admiral snapped. He smacked his fist on the table. "I've been up that river a thousand times in the last seventy years."

Kirk interrupted. "I'm not saying you don't know the way. I know you know the way," he shouted. "I'm saying it's not safe to go, you in a wheelchair, with just her," he indicated Buddy with a jerk of his thumb.

"What you're saying," the Admiral growled, "is that I'm helpless, and she's stupid."

Buddy slumped in her chair and closed her eyes. It was a moment before she felt the Admiral's hand on her shoulder and let herself be pulled out of her chair.

Her grandfather wrapped his arm around her waist. "He's wrong about both of us. We ain't, neither of us, either of those things."

"Don't listen to him," Kirk said. "That isn't what I meant at all." He leaned back in his chair, casually, as if the misunderstanding was settled, but his balance was off. The chairback bumped a notch down the wall, startling him. He swung his arms in a large circle to regain his balance and brought the chair down on its front legs with a jolt.

The Admiral's expression remained cold and angry. He put his arm around Buddy's narrow shoulders, which were humped like she'd been hit in the belly. And when she turned to look at her father, guilt, as if that was exactly what he had meant, swept across Kirk's face. He scraped his chair back and left the kitchen.

"Daddy." Buddy ran after him and caught up just as he was about to shut his bedroom door. "Daddy, it's all right." She stopped when he stopped, lowered her head, and stroked a pine knot with her big toe. "I know I ain't stupid," she said, not looking at him but at the floor. "I just get confused. The Admiral understands 'cause he gets confused, too." Her father was so quiet, she glanced up to see if he was still there, then back at her toe flicking the pine knot. "My feelings ain't hurt."

Kirk stood with his long arms straight at his sides, his head down. He didn't say anything or look at her until the Admiral wheeled up, then he turned, went into his room and closed his door. From within, Buddy thought she heard him say, "I'm sorry."

"Daddy?" she whispered at his door.

"Come with me, honey," the Admiral said. He leaned over and took her hand.

Chapter 10

THE NEXT MORNING WAS SUNDAY. Buddy sat in the stern of the pitpan on her grandmother's milking stool with her hand on the little 7hp Johnston's handle. She was practicing the Admiral's instructions by pretending the motor was running and she was steering.

The Admiral had told her the boat would turn the opposite direction from the way you pushed or pulled the handle. That had sounded just perfect to her.

"Okay," she said to the engine. "I want to go that way." She pointed right then leaned over the stern to watch which way the propeller pointed. She pulled the handle into her stomach then sat for a moment looking between the propeller and her chosen direction. Suddenly, she grinned and smacked the little motor on the back. "We did it," she said. "Let's do it again."

So as not to make it too easy, she straightened the motor first, then chose to go left. She pushed the handle away and leaned over the stern to look. It was perfect. So perfect she felt she'd cheated by just choosing to go the opposite direction. But she felt if she had chosen the same direction, it would have been just as easy. She didn't know how to keep practicing once she'd gotten it right. *Time,* she decided. *I'll do other things to try to forget what I learned.*

Buddy took the gas hose out of the toolbox, attached it to the fuel can, then to the motor. She pumped the bulb exactly three times, pulled the choke out, then stood up and pulled the starter rope as hard as she could. The second time she tried, it started with a rattle and a puff of smoke. She eased off the gas and pushed the choke in.

The pitpan was nosed in beneath the bow of her father's boat and the seawall. Buddy was afraid to try reverse so with the motor in neutral, she untied the bow and the stern lines then, hand over hand, pushed herself down the side of Kirk's boat.

When the pitpan's bow pointed out into the channel, she held her father's stern line while she slowly twisted the handle into forward. Her heart pounded even in her fingertips. The pitpan didn't move. Buddy tried to give it just a little more gas but went too far. The engine roared, and because she was still holding onto the line, the pit-pan's bow swung around and smashed into the back of her father's boat. She twisted the handle back too far the other way, and the motor died.

Her hands were shaking and sweaty. Though she could not find the dent she'd made among the scratches and dents a thousand stone crab traps had made, she still looked around to see if anyone who knew her father had seen her. A boat was coming up the channel, but the docks were empty, except for two men cleaning fish by the boat ramp. She couldn't see them, but she could hear the sounds of fish cleaning: catfish sucking at the surface, the flapping and jostling of pelicans, and the screams of the gulls overhead.

Holding on to a piling, Buddy waited for the incoming boat to pass. It was Miss Conroy, the woman from the dolphin show. Buddy waved then pushed the pitpan around to face the direction she wanted to go.

With the motor carefully notched into neutral, Buddy pushed off the piling and pulled the starter rope. The engine rattled to life. She twisted the handle into forward, then a little further, adding gas. The pitpan puttered down the channel toward the boat ramp. At the ramp, Buddy wanted to go left, but she had forgotten which way to turn the motor. She jerked the handle into her stomach and the boat swung right. She pushed it away too late to miss scraping the seawall on the other side of the canal.

Miss Conroy had backed into a slip two down from the boat ramp and was tying her bowline. She glanced up when Buddy hit the wall. So did the fishermen. Then they all watched her use her hands to push off and line herself up with the ramp. When it was a straight shot, Buddy gave it some gas.

"Cut your motor, little fella," a fisherman called to her.

"I'm not a boy," Buddy said, though not so they could

hear her over the motor, then she twisted the handle the wrong way and roared up the ramp. The propeller gouged into the concrete and stopped.

"You need a mite more practice there, sonny," the second fisherman said, and they laughed.

Jane Conroy gave them a dirty look. "First try?" she asked Buddy.

"Yes, ma'am." Buddy raised the pitpan's motor and jumped out, nearly slipping on the moss. She pulled the boat up the ramp, tied the bowline to a cleat on the seawall, and grinned at Miss Conroy. "My grandfather and me are going up Turner River to see . . ." She stopped and bit her lip. "To fish."

"That's nice."

"I'm Buddy Martin. We live there." She pointed to the house.

"Jane Conroy."

"Yes'm, I remember."

Miss Conroy looked at her, questioningly.

"My teacher, Miss Daniels, says you're studying stone crabs."

"That's right, I am," Jane said, putting a cooler and a toolbox on the dock.

"Well, see ya," Buddy said, turned, and dashed across the road.

She burst into the kitchen. "Admiral, I did it," she shouted, before she saw her father standing at the window over the sink. The water was running and a mound of white foam showed over the rim.

"I'll do those, Daddy," she said, gathering the rest of the breakfast dishes off the table.

"I'll do the dishes, you fix a couple of sandwiches for yourself and Dad, and fill a jar with water." He dropped the last plate into the suds. "I want you to know I'm against this, but I'm not going to stop you. Maybe it'll teach that old coot a lesson."

"Yes, sir. We'll be . . ."

Kirk didn't let her finish. "Seems everybody around here is trying to prove something to someone, whatever the cost." He left the room. The kitchen door made a whooshing sound as it flipped back and forth behind him.

I could catch him, she thought, *catch him and tell him we won't go, or that we wanted him to go, too. But he'd say good, or no.* Buddy raised her arms and twirled around and around, like a coin flipping in the air. When she stopped, she was facing the sink so she did the dishes.

For their lunch she made peanut butter and apple sandwiches—the Admiral's favorite. She wrapped them in wax paper, held in place with rubber bands, and stuffed them into one small paper bag.

Her grandfather had put a list of what they needed to bring with them next to his tackle box by the kitchen door. Buddy read it again. "Fishin nife." Check. "Szisors." Check. "Hamer." Check. "Ribon." From the drawer where her father kept the flashlights and batteries, she took a spool of bright pink plastic ribbon. She put everything in the tackle box with the sandwiches on top, then shut the lid and carried it down to the pitpan.

When the kitchen door slammed behind the Admiral and her father, she had just finishing spraying every crack and crevice, bolt and screw on the little Johnston with WD40. She gave the new oarlocks a quick squirt and put the can away. Neatly laid out in the bottom of the boat were the Admiral's fishing rod, a machete, two oars, a long pole, and the small pile of stakes he had recently cut and painted white. She reached up, took the bucket of shrimp off the seawall and put it next to his tackle box.

The Admiral rolled his chair down the kitchen ramp and crunched along the crushed oystershell road to the docks. Kirk hopped over the railing. Both their chins jutted forward and their jaws were tight.

At the top of the boat ramp, the Admiral stopped and sat grimly with his elbows on the armrests. Kirk lifted him out of the chair, swung around, and without great care, deposited him on the seawall. He snatched up the chair with one hand, stomped down the ramp, and jammed its wheels between the wooden blocks.

Jane, who was washing down her boat, looked over her shoulder, folded the hose to stop the water, and watched.

Buddy smiled at her. "This is my grandfather," she said. "Admiral, this here's Miss Conroy. The lady from the dolphin show."

"Ah ha," Jane said, apparently realizing where Buddy remembered her from.

Kirk looked around in surprise, then put his hands on his hips. "Well, well. We have a new boat in the fleet. Are you for charter, Miss Conroy?"

She lifted her chin and glared at him.

Kirk gave a short laugh, turned, slipped on the wet moss, spun on his rear, and slid backward into the canal.

Buddy and Jane laughed until he came up sputtering. Buddy took a deep breath and held it. Jane turned her back and released the hose.

Kirk came out of the water on his hands and knees. "I wish I'd been carrying you, you old goat," he snarled up at his father, who had fallen back on the path laughing.

"I know," the Admiral said, and laughed all the harder.

"Stop it," Buddy said to her father.

He did, and her grandfather sat up, and Jane turned around again.

"It's not funny anymore," Buddy said, staring at the place in the ramp where a chunk of concrete was missing.

Two and a half years ago, the Admiral had been standing on that very spot on the ramp holding a friend's bowline when the boat a tourist was hauling out broke its cable and slid off the trailer. A fisherman on the dock shouted a warning, and the Admiral spun in time to see the boat lurch toward him. He tried to jump clear but, like Kirk, his feet skidded on the moss-covered concrete and he slid on his back down the ramp. Everyone agreed that if he'd dropped off into the canal, he would have been all right, but he stopped himself by grabbing a trailer tire and tried to roll in tight against it. The vee of the bow caught him on his left side at his waist, crushing his spine.

"It's all right, honey," her grandfather said. "My accident was too long ago not to have a good laugh on your pa."

He was still grinning when Kirk got him around the waist and slung him over his shoulder like a sack of flour, then flipped him into his chair and pushed them off, leaving a wide scrape of fresh red paint on the ramp. The pit-pan drifted to the side of the canal and bumped gently against the seawall.

Buddy twisted the handle into neutral, stood up and jerked the starter rope. The motor sputtered to life. She looked back toward the ramp just as the kitchen door slammed behind her father.

The Admiral twisted in his chair, glanced at the house, then smiled at her. "Okay, Captain, dead ahead." He turned and swung his arm like a general leading troops into battle.

Buddy waved good-bye to Miss Conroy, straightened the motor and eased the handle around to forward.

Chapter 11

SLOWLY THEY PUTTERED beneath the faded No Wake sign toward the end of the canal. As they approached the channel, Buddy saw the Admiral tighten his grip on the armrests. She turned to check the prop then twisted the engine a little one way, then the other, before making a flawless left turn into the channel.

"What a seaman," her grandfather hooted.

The breeze off the Gulf was fresh and warm. The Admiral put his head back, took a deep breath, then spread his arms wide. "Smell that," he said. "Just smell that air."

At the end of channel, Buddy swung them left past Smallwood's store, then on around the eastern edge of the island. From there less than a half mile of choppy bay separated them from the wide mouth of Turner River, but the Admiral pointed left.

"Go around and cross on the lee side of the causeway," he called back to her. "Out of the wind where the water's calm."

Once in the river, she eased off the gas, opened the

tackle box, and took out the pink plastic ribbon and the scissors. Carefully, she stepped forward and handed them to her grandfather.

As she steered them upriver, he measured ten strips the length of his forearm and cut them.

Where the river narrowed and turned rust-colored, the flow of the tide became less noticeable. And then, around a bend, the river looked as if it ended.

"There's a tunnel there somewhere," he said, scanning the wall of mangroves.

"There?" she said, pointing off to the left.

"No, that ain't it. That dead-ends. Look at the water. It's scummy and stagnant 'cause it ain't flowing nowhere. That's how you tell. Got it?"

"Yes, sir." She grinned and saluted him.

"I see it." He pointed to the right. "Ease her into the opening so I can cut those branches back. It may be too overgrown to get through, but we don't know 'til we try."

After he cleared away the branches that blocked the entrance, he drove a white stake into the mud at the side of the opening to the tunnel and tied a pink ribbon around at the notch he'd made in the top. "Your first marker," he said, and smiled at her over his shoulder.

The tangled branches of red mangroves, with their high arching prop roots, closed over their heads, plunging the river into cool darkness. They weren't all the way into the dark channel when the mosquitoes discovered them.

"You want some spray?" she asked, taking a can of 6-12 from the tackle box.

"Naw, I don't feel them anymore. My hide's too tough."

Buddy wished her hide was tough because she hated the smell of mosquito spray. She took her cap off, held her breath, squeezed her eyes shut, and sprayed herself from head to toe, then aimed a cloud of spray at the Admiral before putting the can away.

The tunnel wound and twisted through the mangroves. They moved slowly so the Admiral could cut away the low branches, and they stopped when they came to an opening large enough for her to doubt which way to go. He showed her how to watch the current. "The strongest flow is the main stream," he said, but drove a stake and tied a ribbon to mark it anyway.

If they had been coming from the other direction, the place where they broke out of the tunnel and into sunlight was indistinguishable from any other dent in the wall of mangroves. The river, when she looked back, appeared to flow straight south between a bank of cattails on one side and the mangroves on the other.

Her grandfather carefully marked out the entrance with stakes on either side and a ribbon streaming from the branches above it. When he was finished, he turned and grinned at her. "It's downhill now. Fifty more yards and we turn off onto the main track across the prairie. It's a straight shot from there."

The sawgrass prairie was scarred with airboat trails and pocked with cattail stands, which encircled holes scraped out by alligators during winter dry-downs.

When they were about a hundred yards away from Stevens's, Buddy heard an airboat coming. Before she could think of where to go to get out of its way, it burst onto the trail just in front of them, made a sliding left turn and roared away toward Stevens's dock. The blast from its propeller blew the pitpan's bow around nearly tipping the Admiral over backward, and might have if he hadn't leaned into its wind.

"I hate them things," he muttered. "See those willows?" He pointed to the small stand of trees growing up the levee on the riverside. The pipe from the dolphins' pond jutted out of the embankment just behind them.

"Yes, sir," she said.

"If you pull in there, we'll be out of that jackass's way."

Buddy grinned to herself. She was tapping a bare foot on the floor of the pitpan as if she heard music.

Chapter 12

A FEW FEET SHORT OF THE LEVEE, Buddy cut the motor and let them drift into the willows. She waited until the Admiral tied them up with the bowline, then she poled the stern around parallel to the levee, jammed the pole into the mud, and tied the stern line to it.

"Hand me that fishing rod and the shrimp bucket before you go visiting, will ya?"

"I wish you could see them," she said, passing the bait bucket to him.

"I've seen a thousand dolphins," he said.

For a minute, she stood watching him bait his hook.

"Go on now," he said. "I'm happy as a pelican under a cleaning stand." He held his hand out to steady her as she stepped from the pitpan onto the side of the levee.

At the top, she waved to him, then crossed to the sea grape tree, stepped down and straddled the drain pipe.

The pond was smooth, empty looking. She stood up amid the branches and peered over at the show pool, but it was quiet there, too.

"Hello, dolphins?" she called softly.

A sucking sound came from the pipe as a swell moved the garbage caught against the metal bars. It was a moment or two before she realized the movement of the brown water was caused by a passing dolphin. By then the pond was still again.

A palmetto frond floated amid gum wrappers, plastic ice bags, beer and Coke bottles, and two dead fish. Buddy got on her stomach, reached into the trash and lifted the long frond out. The rotted leafy part dropped off leaving only the paddle-shaped end of the stalk. She used this to scoop the garbage away and shovel it up onto the bank beside the pipe.

She worked a while, before she saw the circle of gray cheek and the eye watching her. She smiled at it. "Hi," she said, and kept cleaning.

More of the dolphin's head appeared until she could see the smile-shaped curve of its mouth.

"I figured if I cleaned this drain out, you'd get some nicer water in here."

She had stirred up a stink. Pinching her nose closed, she reached between the bars and pulled out a giant tangle of fishing line along with all the moss that had grown around it. The drain made a gurgling sound, then a loud sucking noise before water from the pond swept through, belching the remaining trash into the water behind the pitpan.

"There," she said, sat up and wiped her hands on her shorts. "I suppose you don't remember me. I was here two weeks ago on my birthday."

The smile and eye sank out of sight.

"No, I suppose you don't," Buddy said, and dipped her toes in the rush of water through the pipe. "I guess I oughta go say hi to Mr. Blossom," she said, after the pond had been still for a while.

Just as she was about to stand, a dolphin popped up in front of her.

"You scared me." She laughed, sat down again and put her toes back in the water. "My grandfather marked a trail for me so I can come up to see you anytime. He's just over there now—fishing." She jerked her thumb in his direction. "He would've come over, but he can't walk."

The slick gray face smiled at her.

"You're Annie, right? I'm Buddy. Buddy Martin. From Chokoloskee. Right down the river." She pointed out the direction for the dolphin. It bobbed its head and squeaked.

Buddy giggled. The dolphin bobbed again then squeezed a whistling sound and a couple of pops from its blowhole.

One of the other dolphins surfaced nearby, expelled air and disappeared. As if they were connected to one another, her dolphin disappeared, too.

Buddy found O. B. Stevens leaning across the bottom half of the door to the ticket booth, talking quietly to, and rubbing the shoulder of, a pretty girl.

"Mr. Blossom," Buddy said softly and touched his arm.

He jumped. "Yeah, what do you want?"

"I'm Buddy Martin. Remember?"

"Who?"

"Kirk Martin's daughter."

"Oh yeah. The birthday girl. Where's your pa?" He glanced toward the parking lot.

"He ain't with me. My grandfather brought me."

"The Admiral? Where is that old codger?"

"In the boat."

"What boat?"

"The pitpan. In the river."

"You two came up the river?"

"Yes, sir."

"Ain't he still in a wheelchair?"

Buddy nodded.

Stevens sucked at his teeth making a sound like the catfish at the docks, then snorted a laugh. "If that don't beat all. What are you two doing here?"

"I came up to see the dolphins again."

Stevens stuck a short pinky into his mouth and scraped at a back tooth. "Well, okay," he said, flicking whatever he'd gotten off his finger. "You want me to send some boys to get that crazy grandpa of yours out of the boat? We got another show in about ten minutes. I'll only charge for the old man. You can go in free."

"No, sir. Thank you anyway. I've already been to see them. We gotta be heading back."

"You were in the last show?"

"No, sir. I went and sat by their pond to watch them."

Stevens jammed his cigar in his mouth and rolled it

around. "That there's a no trespassing area. Folks ain't allowed down there."

Buddy ducked her head. Her toes began working at the gravel. "I'm sorry," she said, "I didn't mean to trespass."

"It's because of the snakes. Pygmy rattlers is around there. You stay away from there from now on."

"Yes, sir." Buddy started to back away then stopped.

Stevens was leaning in the door again.

"Mr. Blossom? I only saw two dolphins."

He looked over his shoulder. "Osceola's dead."

Buddy's eyes were on Stevens's lip. It glistened like a wound. "How come?" she whispered. "How come?" Her voice cracked.

Stevens patted her head. "He was old, kid. That's all." He turned back to the girl in the booth. "I'll talk to you later." He winked at her, then rocked away.

Buddy stepped over the chain with the No Trespassing sign still dangling by one hook. She looked back in time to see Stevens go through the gate to the show pool. Balling her hands into fists, she shouted: "Miss Conroy told you he was sick."

He didn't hear her, but the girl in the booth peered out.

Buddy picked up a chunk of limestone and threw it as hard as she could at the sign. It missed. She ran at it and kicked it. The sign broke loose and spun away across the gravel lot.

Chapter 13

"ADMIRAL." BUDDY STOOD ON THE LEVEE above the pitpan, hiked her arm and wiped her eyes on her shoulder.

"What's wrong, sweetie?"

"Osceola's dead."

"Oh, honey, I'm sorry." He held his arms out.

"Miss Conroy was right. She said he was killing them." Buddy came down the levee to let him hug her. Over his shoulder she saw the stringer. "Did you get some fish?"

"Yep. Three snook. Nice ones, too." He leaned over and pulled them in.

"Can I have two of them?"

"Well, yeah, I guess so. One of them ain't all that big, and this one here you and me can share." He took off the biggest fish and handed her the stringer. "We'll give them dolphins your pa's share." He grinned.

Buddy crossed the levee, swung down onto the pipe and patted the surface of the water. A flat, slick paw print appeared in front of her. "Annie? I brought you a fresh fish. The Admiral just caught it." She slipped the larger of the two remaining snook off the stringer, got a good grip on its tail, then held it out to the dolphin.

Annie upended and stood with her whole head out of the water, but made no move to take the fish.

"Please, Annie. It's fresh." She wiggled it in the air. "See, it's still alive."

Annie moved closer and brushed the fish lightly with her snout.

A whistle blew, and the scratchy Lone Ranger's theme came over the loudspeakers. The dolphin disappeared.

Buddy carefully put the fish back on the stringer. "Don't you die, Annie," she said softly. "Please, don't you die."

"I don't see how he's allowed to keep them if he don't feed them right." Buddy handed the stringer back to the Admiral. She stepped into the pitpan, jerked the lines loose from the willows, and rocked the pole angrily until it came loose, then she pushed them off and out into the river. The southward flow caught and floated them quickly downstream, stern first.

"Always start your motor first, honey," the Admiral said, "before you untie, in case it don't start. Now you got no control over where you're going." He spoke calmly, and smiled over his shoulder at her, but his grip was tight on the armrests.

Buddy yanked the starter rope over and over. "Admiral?"

"It's okay, honey. Take it easy. We're going to lodge in them reeds there, see?"

They drifted sideways into a stand of sawgrass. The Admiral grabbed a handful of the sharp-sided grass and held on. "Let the starter rope wind in all the way, then pull it."

The little motor fired with a roar, plunging them forward toward the mountain of trash rising out of the weeds at the end of the levee.

Buddy fell across the engine hood.

"Honey!" the Admiral shouted. "Turn!"

With one hand on either side of the cowling, she was pushing herself upright when he yelled his warning. She twisted the motor. The pitpan made a sweeping arc away from the embankment and back out into the river.

"Well, I'll be dipped," the Admiral said, and laughed. "You saved us. Guess you'll remember to make sure you're in neutral next time. Huh?"

"I'm sorry, Admiral. Maybe Daddy was right."

"Oh bull. I made plenty of mistakes when I was learning. I ran my pa's boat aground so many times, he gave me a hoe one Christmas. Said I spent so much time on dry land, I might as well plant something."

"Is that true?" She grinned.

"Word of honor," he raised his right hand.

"Admiral, your hand's all bloody."

"Couple of little scratches. Ain't nothing. Shows my hide's getting soft." He wiped his hands on his pants and used his shirttail to clean the blood off the armrests of his chair.

83

"You want your sandwich yet?" Buddy asked when they were out of sight of Stevens.

"Pretty soon, now. There's a secret lagoon I want to show you."

"Where you used to go with the Indians?"

"An Indian showed it to me, but I 'spect I'm the only man alive, white or red, still knows where it is. It ain't easy to find. Even back then, the way to it was only wide enough for a dugout," he said, then set his cap low against the sun.

Buddy added gas slowly until they were clipping along. At the pink-ribboned stake marking the airboat trail, she slowed and turned off the shallow track onto the river, spooking a Great Blue heron. He flew downstream ahead of them with great sweeping strokes, his passing shadow alarming schools of mullet, which exploded into the air with each downward beat.

"Nice, huh?" the Admiral called over his shoulder.

"Yes, sir," she said dully. It was hard to feel any enthusiasm for what was left of the day.

"Go past our tunnel about a hundred yards," the Admiral said, "then slow up so I can watch for the opening to the lagoon." A couple minutes later he pointed. "I think that's it on the right. See it?"

Where he pointed looked like nothing more than a deep dent in the mangroves to her. "You sure that's it, Admiral?"

"Wouldn't be a secret lagoon if it could be found easy."

Her grandfather cut away the limbs blocking the entrance, then tied a ribbon just inside. "You'll have to look to see this one, but it'll keep anybody else from finding it."

The tunnel was short and narrow with a bend in the middle that made it look, once inside, as if it had closed behind them. At the end it ballooned into a small lagoon with shellmounds rising up from its shores.

Chokoloskee was mostly shellmounds, but all the building since the bridge and causeway to the mainland went in had obscured or flattened them. These were the first she'd ever seen without a gas station or a motel on top.

"My teacher says the Calusa Indians built the shellmounds for high ground in hurricanes. Is that true, Admiral?"

"No it ain't." He shook his head. "Hurricanes didn't bother the Calusas none. They had hurricane savvy. They built their houses on stilts, which took a lot less effort than piling up oyster shells just for some place high enough to sit out a blow.

"Now the Seminoles weren't any smarter than we are. When they drove the Calusas off, they burned their houses. Next hurricane that hit, they had to skedaddle up Turner River and ride it out in the mangroves. You can tell that hotshot, know-it-all, Yankee teacher of yours that she don't know her rear end from a bait chute."

"Well, I probably won't tell her that." Buddy grinned.

"No, guess not." He laughed. "But you can tell her that I said they didn't build those mounds for no purpose, they just shucked a lot of oysters in 3,000 years. Ask her what she thinks they was doing about hurricanes the first thousand years while they was waiting for the mounds to get some height?"

"Oh, look, Admiral." Buddy pointed to six Roseate spoonbills, plastic-ribbon pink, that had moved into sight on the far side of the lagoon. They looked up briefly, then, as if they had decided the distance between was safe, went back to sweeping their bills through the muck for food.

Buddy cut the motor and poled the pitpan along the edge to a shady spot in the mangroves. She tied the stern line to a thick prop root, then climbed across them to the front and took the bowline from the Admiral. She hunkered on the roots when she was done tying and took the sandwich he passed her.

"Admiral, you ever wished you was something different than you are?"

"Yep, bunches of times. Right now, I wish I was forty years younger and didn't have this chair attached to my butt." He reached and touched her knee. "Do you wish you was something else?"

"Uh-huh." She looked at him, her brow furrowed. "I wish I was a bird or a dolphin or growed or something that didn't have to go to school Monday—or ever again."

"Would you feel different if Alex was a snook on that stringer?"

"Yep. That would help." She grinned. "You know what?" She was watching the spoonbills. "Mr. Blossom's got a bottom lip that's the same shape as a spoonbill's bill."

"I remember." He wiped peanut butter off her cheek.

The level of water in the long, narrow tunnel was lower on the way home. In a few places, the receding tide left half moons of reddish mud, glistening wetly, and covered with weblike shadows cast by the light that seeped through the branches above. Buddy slowed for each one and carefully nosed the pitpan into the flow around them.

"Tide's gone out," her grandfather said, yawned, then let his head droop onto his chest.

The tide had not gone out enough to expose the corner of a rusted washing machine that had settled into the muck. They hit it with a dull clunk. The Admiral started awake and gripped the armrests as the pitpan's bow scraped over it, lifted and tipped his chair. He tried to lean the other way, but he was too late and up too high. The chair lay over but stayed in the boat. The Admiral fell out and disappeared beneath the surface.

"Admiral," Buddy shrieked and swung the pitpan wildly to miss him. The stern swept around until the motor's prop hit a mangrove root and stopped. She leapt over the side and waded, armpit-deep, upstream against the flow. Twice she tripped on silt-covered branches or roots, fell and was washed back a few yards.

The Admiral floated on the surface, his useless legs pointed downstream. He had hooked his right arm around a prop root, the other arm swept back and forth freely in the current. His eyes were squeezed shut and his lips were pulled back over his dentures in a grimace.

When she reached his side, she caught his left hand. He yelled in pain then moaned. "I think it's broke," he said quietly.

She moved around behind him with the intention of trying to lift him higher onto the roots, but she was afraid to touch his arm again. She tried to pull him up by his belt, which must have startled him into thinking he was losing his grip on the root.

"Don't," he yelled.

"Help me," she cried out. "Please, somebody help me."

"No good calling, honey," he moaned. "There ain't nobody around to hear you. I'm okay. I've got a good hold on this root. You go get the boat and bring it here."

"Admiral, please let me help you."

"Go get the boat, Buddy. That's how you can help me."

She tried to run but the water was too deep. The mud sucked at her feet. She started swimming, her arms beating the water. But every few strokes she looked back to make sure he was still there.

The pitpan had drifted around a bend and lodged among the mangroves fifty yards downstream. She climbed out into the trees and stepped down into the boat. Every root looked like the one he'd been clinging to, but she could not see him. Panic swept over her. She jerked on the cord and the engine started, lurched across into the mangroves on the other side of the river, and stalled. But she could see him then.

She put it in neutral and let the stern swing downstream before starting the engine again. His white hair, now reddening with tannic silt, was her beacon.

When she was a yard or two away, she cut the motor, jumped overboard, and tied the bowline to a branch just above his head.

"You're gonna have to leave me here," he said.

"I can't leave you, Admiral."

"You have to. I can't get back in the boat with no legs and only one arm."

"I'll help you."

"You can't lift me." His voice was harsh with pain. "You do what I tell you."

"Yes, sir."

"Get my chair and put it here as near me as you can."

She got it and put it in the water. It upended and started downstream. She grabbed it and tried to jam it in among the roots. They were too dense and gnarled.

"Untie the stern line."

She laid the chair back in the bow and waded along the side of the pitpan until she could reach and untie the rope.

When she waded back to him, his eyes were closed. "Admiral?" She touched his cheek and held the rope up for him to see.

"That's my girl." He tried to smile. "Tie one end to a good strong root. That's it. Is it tight?"

She pulled on it as hard as she could.

"Good. Now get the chair and loop the rope once

around the strut just beneath the backrest, then bring the rope around my waist."

She put the wheelchair in the mud, just behind and beneath the Admiral's head. The seat pointed downstream. She looped the rope through it and around his waist. With her other hand, she lifted and floated him into a sitting position in the chair.

"That's it, that's it," he said, moving his grip up the root he had been holding. "Loop it around the other strut. Now, pull me into the chair.

"Make the rope tighter," he yelled, when she let go and the current caught him, sliding him down in the chair.

She pulled it tight, waded behind him, and looped the rope through another root as he instructed. "Now pull me in tight. As hard as you can." He let go of the root to help her pull.

When they had it tight, the chair tilted backward, then slid down until it rested at an angle in the mud. The Admiral grabbed a branch over his head, then cautiously, let it go. The chair shifted, but held. The water came to his armpits.

"Admiral, your neck's bleeding." She touched the tear in his shirt near the collar and felt the jagged tip of his clavicle. He flinched. Blood seeped from the wound, spread down his chest and swirled away when it reached the water sweeping around him.

He surveyed himself. "I'm pretty banged up, ain't I?" He patted her arm. "Hand me them napkins out of the tackle box then get going. We ain't got a lot of time, honey, before the tide turns."

Buddy felt suddenly sick to her stomach. "How long?"

"Plenty of time for you to get help. Go slow and be careful. Okay?"

She nodded because she couldn't speak.

"Leave me my fishing knife. If the water gets too high, I'll cut myself loose and hug a root 'til you get here." He grinned at her. "If your pa ain't in yet, and I kinda hope he ain't, get Raffield or one of the Browns to come back with you."

"Admiral, can't I just wait here with you until somebody comes by?"

"Honey, nobody uses this river any more. Leastways not up this far, and it'll be dark in three hours. The trail's marked, and I promise to wait right here for you." He smiled, put his good arm around her neck and pulled her head to his cheek. "I'm a tough old coot, honey. This will all work out. You go on now."

"I'm sorry, Admiral."

He shook a finger in her face. "Don't you go trying to blame yourself for this." He lifted her chin. "It was my own fault. I was suppose to be watching and I dozed off." He kissed her. "Now git."

She climbed in the pitpan and started the motor. When she stepped forward to untie the bowline, he made an okay circle with his thumb and forefinger. "This here is some adventure we're having, ain't it, honey?"

"Yes, sir." Smiling for him then was the hardest thing she'd ever done.

She watched him waving until she turned the bend. A half mile downstream, she slowed, leaned over and lifted his Mack truck cap out of where the mangrove roots had trapped it. She took hers off and put his on. Water poured down her neck and into her ears. She looked up through the overhanging branches. "Momma, please watch him for me."

Chapter 14

AFTER WHAT SEEMED LIKE ALL THE YEARS of her life so far, Buddy at last saw the end of the river open up and Chokoloskee on the horizon. And when the bow smacked into the choppy waters of the bay, she felt a rush of relief just to hold steady. She pointed the pitpan straight across and let the spray on her face and the fear of capsizing keep all her other terrors under control.

The momentary rush of joy she felt at seeing her father loading his crab traps onto the stern of his boat was as great as the anguish that swept over her when he looked up and saw her coming into the channel. His face went white.

From the pay phone on the docks, Kirk called Naples for an ambulance to meet them at Stevens's. And since the pitpan was the only boat small enough to make it through the narrow parts of the river, they raced up the highway with it in the bed of the truck.

Though Buddy kept her eyes focused on the road, she

could still see her father's jaw, tight as a fist. The air in the cab of the truck felt like soup in her lungs, yet she was afraid to breathe too loudly or too deeply for fear of calling his attention to the fact that she was there.

The speed with which they came off the road and into the parking lot at Stevens's created a cloud of white dust. Her father leaped into the heart of it. "You stay here," he shouted and slammed the door.

"No, Daddy, please." She jumped out. "Let me go with you."

"No," he snapped, dragging the pitpan by its stern from the bed of the truck. He ran, pulling it behind him by the bowline, to the airboat dock where he shoved it into the water.

"You don't know where he is," Buddy said.

"He's the only old man in a wheelchair out there, isn't he?" he snapped, then glared at her. "But he's not the only person who knows that river." He stepped in and pushed the pitpan away from the dock.

"Start your motor first," she whispered, swiping at her tears with the heel of her hand.

For a half hour, Buddy sat on top of the trash heap watching the sawgrass prairie for a sign of them. When the airboat returned from its tour, she told the driver what had happened. After a phone call, probably to Stevens for permission, he headed downriver then swept east onto the prairie.

About fifteen minutes later, over the scratchy, sickening sound of the Lone Ranger theme, Buddy began to hear the far-off wail of the ambulance and then, from the

94

other direction, the muted roar of an airboat. She waited till she could see him then jumped down and ran the levee to the docks.

The Admiral was lying on the front bench. He waved to her and smiled.

"I still hate these damn noisy things," he muttered as the ambulance and airboat drivers lifted him onto the stretcher.

"Your father said for you to ride with him," the airboat driver said, jerking his thumb toward her grandfather. "When and if he gets here in that little thing, he'll follow."

"What did your father say?" the Admiral asked, over the wail of the siren. The hand she held, like the rest of him, was caked with mud.

"Nothing," she said. "I think he was too mad to talk."

"Well, I wish he'd stayed that way for my part of the ride with him." They had given him a shot; a sedative. His eyes were closed. "He chewed on me like tough steak as long as he had me."

"How high was the tide when he found you?" Buddy asked.

"Only to my chin," he said and grinned sleepily. "All the time in the world . . ."

"He's really gonna hate us now," she said.

The Admiral opened his eyes and rolled his head to look at her. "You're wrong, honey. As much as I hate to admit it, this was never about him not liking us, it's about him liking us too much. He just don't know how to do it right."

~   ~   ~

For as long as Buddy could remember, her grandfather sat at the end of the kitchen table with his back to the window. The few times she'd come running late to the house for dinner, his silver hair had shone there like a warm light. The evening of the day he came home from the hospital, she wheeled him to his place.

"I want to sit at the other end," he said.

Kirk turned from the fish he was frying. "You've always sat there."

"Not anymore," he snapped. "I want to see out."

Buddy backed him around and looked at her father.

"I got a thousand things left to do to get ready for tomorrow and you want me to add rearranging furniture to the list because you're feeling sorry for yourself."

"Speaking of self-pity," the Admiral said.

"Yeah," Kirk sneered. "Well as long as I'm the only one feeding us and keeping a roof over our heads, I've got the right to gripe."

The Admiral looked up at his son. "Speaking for your burdens . . ." Buddy's hand was on his bandaged shoulder, he covered it with his own. ". . . I'd like to apologize for the inconvenience we are to you."

"That's not what I'm saying," Kirk snapped. "I'm suggesting at some point you might give me a little consideration."

"I want to watch the bay," the Admiral said. "Is that too much to ask? To at least be able to *see* the water."

"Oh bull." Kirk took the frying pan off the stove and walked to the table. The Admiral glared up at him.

Kirk's expression hardened to match his father's. He roughly shoved the little table up against the window frame. With the side of his arm, he dragged the salt, pepper, and Tabasco down to the other end, then rolled his father's knife and fork in his napkin and delivered them to him like a diploma.

"There." Kirk stood back, his hands folded across his chest to survey the new setup. "Does that suit you?"

"That will do it," the Admiral snapped, unrolling his napkin and jamming a corner into the edge of the bandage around his chest.

Kirk turned away and slapped the frying pan back on the burner. "Maybe you're right," he said. "From the looks of you, watching is all you're suited for and what you should stick with."

There was a sudden silence in the room. Even the fish he'd been frying hadn't started to sizzle again yet.

Buddy felt the sting of her father's words, but her heart jumped when she saw her grandfather's expression. The muscles in his face had gone slack and his eyes were listless like a fish landed after the fight is lost. She got up from her new place at the table and went to stand with him. "That's not true," she whispered.

Her father straightened at the stove and he turned to glance over his shoulder. He must have seen what he'd done, too, because his brow creased and he said: "Something's got to snap you out of this." He turned back to the stove, flipped the fish, then said: "You two want to go with me in the morning?"

Buddy knew her father didn't really want them, that this was his way of apologizing, but she smiled at her grandfather. "Want to, Admiral?"

"I'd be in the way," he said.

"I need you to run the boat," Kirk said.

"Yeah, Admiral, you can steer. Daddy can pull 'em, and I'll . . ." For a minute, she couldn't think of anything left for her to do. "I could bait 'em," she said finally.

"No," her grandfather said, taking the napkin from the neck of his bandage. He tried to roll himself away from the table, but he couldn't without help.

"Please, Admiral."

For a moment his eyes sparked. "If I'm in the way here at my own damn table, I sure ain't going out on that boat now that it's his."

"Jesus," Kirk muttered, jammed a spatula under the cooked fish, slapped it onto a plate, and brought it to his father.

"I'm not hungry," the Admiral said.

"You haven't eaten since yesterday. The nurse told me." Kirk picked up his father's napkin and tucked it back into his bandage.

The Admiral snatched it out again. "I'm still your father; don't tell me what to do."

"Eat, damn it, or I take you back to the hospital and let them feed you through a tube."

The Admiral glared at Kirk then grabbed the Tabasco and doused the fish with it. He tore off a piece with his fork and jammed it into his mouth.

"I'd miss school if we went with you tomorrow," Buddy said. She wanted this to stop.

"It's the first day of the season, a lot of kids will miss tomorrow. They're needed on the boats."

"Okay then," she said, not believing for a minute that he really wanted her to go. "I'll be there. How 'bout it, Admiral?"

As if he hadn't heard her, he pushed his plate away. "I should have been sitting here all along," he said, staring out at the darkness beyond the window.

Chapter 15

THE NEXT MORNING Buddy came down to the docks at five-thirty, rubbing her eyes and yawning. The day was already warm and humid, though the sun was not yet up. The only light came from a bare bulb hanging from the ceiling of the trunk cabin of her father's boat. He had the engine running and the cover off, checking the bilge pump.

She waited until he slid the cover back across the opening. "Morning," she said, covering another yawn with the back of her hand.

"You all set?"

Buddy wondered about that herself. This was the first year he had ever asked her to help, and she was pretty sure it wasn't because he thought she'd really be any. "Yes, sir," she said anyway, then asked, "It's still okay if I go, isn't it?"

"Yeah," he said, then looked up at her. "Sure it is." He reached up and she stepped off into his hands.

Her father always pulled traps from the starboard side of the stern. He had already put all his equipment within reach. Leaning against the starboard gunnel was the broom handle with a large hook driven into one end that he used to snag the buoy lines. On his right were buckets full of fish heads, skins, and other scraps. It was called stinking bait, and it did. Next to the bait buckets were three large, green, plastic bins, stacked atop each other.

From the darkness beyond Kirk's light came the crunch of tires stopping on gravel. A door slammed and another crabber stepped out of the morning blackness.

Soon more men appeared. An engine started further down the dock, then another. Diesel fuel, cigarette smoke, and the smell of bait blended with, then edged out, the heavy smell of the sea.

Chokoloskee's sky had a high, thin, gauzy layer of clouds, but far to the south, lightning flickered silently through spiraling thunderheads.

"Cast off the bowline when I tell you, okay?"

"Yes, sir." She smiled at him, then stepped up and edged along the port gunnel to the bow.

Kirk untied the crossed stern lines. "Okay," he called.

The line was taut. Buddy struggled with it, then pulled the boat forward for slack, untied the line, looped it neatly, and laid it on the dock.

"No, no." Kirk came along the gunnel. "We need to have the rope with us." He jumped the gap between the bow and the dock, grabbed the coil of rope and tossed it to her. "Retie it," he said.

Buddy looped her end of the rope back and forth in a figure eight over the arms of the cleat.

"That'll do it," Kirk said, then pulled the boat tight to the dock, untied his end of line and stepped back aboard with it.

"I'm sorry," she said as he went past her. "I guess I forgot."

"It's okay."

Kirk eased the boat away from the docks and out into the channel. Buddy stayed forward. Before he turned it off, the light in the trunk cabin made the water look like old, cold coffee. When the blackness settled over them, she leaned back against the cabin bulkhead and rolled the end of the bowline around her palm. Its rough, scratchy texture was like a calloused hand to hold in the thick still darkness. Her hair and face were damp from the humidity. She ran her arm across her forehead, put her head back against the bulkhead, closed her eyes, and fell asleep to the subtle throb of the engine and the rush of water against their bow.

A half hour later, they came out of Chokoloskee Pass into the dead calm waters of Florida Bay. The churning and splashing in water to her left woke her. She sat up and squinted into the gray dawn. "Daddy. Look." She stood and pointed toward the exposed mudbank of a mangrove island. "There's a beached dolphin. Do you see him?"

"He's not beached," Kirk said, slowing the engine and swinging the bow around toward the island. "He's fishing."

As they neared, the dolphin humped itself back into the water and disappeared. A moment later, a fin broke the surface, then a second one, and they began crossing back and forth off the beach until the shallow water boiled with fish. When they had driven a mass of them onto the bank, the two dolphins nosed into the mud, rolled a little to one side, and picked off their catch, one by one.

"I can't believe they can do that," Buddy said.

Kirk laughed. "Looks like they can to me."

It was still over an hour's run to her father's first line. The sun was up, its rays knifing through gaps in the storm clouds. Only their wake disturbed the calmness of the water, now a pale shade of rose.

Just past Indian Key, Buddy spotted their first buoy.

Kirk had 450 traps out in three lines, dropped in different parts of the bay. He'd pull 150 traps a day for the next three, then wait a few days before starting all over again. He did this all season, October 15 to May 15.

Carlisle Townsend, Alex's father, had nearly a thousand traps out. But he could afford to hire help. All he had to do anymore was steer a course between the rows of traps while the pullers, one on either side of the stern, did the work Buddy's father did alone.

Because he pulled alone, her father's lines were in single rows of seventy-five traps each. One half started just ahead, the other half was a quarter mile west, too far for her to see the string of small buoys.

Kirk slowed and rapped on the port wall of the cabin for her attention. When she looked around the edge, he crooked a finger for her to come.

103

"You're going to run the boat," he said, when she hopped off the gunnel beside him.

"I am?"

He smiled and nodded. "It's a straight line," he said. "Just watch the markers and do what I tell you."

"Yes, sir." She was very nervous.

Stretching out before them was the row of styrofoam mannequin heads her father used as buoys to mark the location of each trap. Their faces were pink in the morning sun. Black nylon ropes ran from the end of the trap, up through their necks, and out the top of their heads like double-strand ponytails. The first one in line had a barnacle on her chin and chunks missing from her face, pecked away by gulls.

"When I hook the buoy, put the engine in neutral," Kirk instructed, then leaned over with the broom handle and snagged the line to the trap just below the mannequin's neck. When he had it within reach, he put the broom handle down, grabbed the rope, then hand over hand, hauled the sixty-five-pound trap up through the soupy water and lifted it onto the stern. "When the trap's here," he said, "put the engine in forward. That way we'll be on our way to the next trap while I'm emptying this one. You don't need to touch the throttle. Okay?"

Buddy nodded and wiped her damp palms on the seat of her shorts. Her heart pounded in her chest as she took the wheel.

"Go ahead," he said. "Put it in forward."

She eased it into gear. They moved slowly ahead.

Kirk turned the catch and lifted the lid of the trap. "Four," he muttered. "One's a short and one's female. Gravid," he said, holding the female up for her to see. A mass of orange eggs covered the back of her abdomen. He dropped the under legal-sized short and the female over the side. The other two were big males, called boars. He tossed them into the nearest green plastic, rectangular tub, scooped up a fistful of fish scraps, stuffed them down the cylindrical steel bait chute, slammed and latched the lid. He shoved the trap over, then checked the position of the buoy they were approaching.

They must have been too far from it, because Kirk reached around her, jerked the wheel hard right, then straightened it before he leaned to hook the buoy's rope. "Stop."

Buddy put it in neutral.

"Good," he said, pulling the trapline in, hand over hand. "Got it. Go."

She moved the gear into forward and leaned over to watch for the next buoy.

"Seven," he said, "and a blue crab and a snapper." He pitched the blue crab and a female stone crab over and handed her the snapper. "Dinner. Put it in the fish box."

She held it by the tail with one hand and steered with the other. When it was time to put it in neutral again, she darted forward, threw the fish in on the ice and dashed back to the wheel.

The bottom of the first green box was covered with stone crabs by the seventh trap, which came up with two of its sides torn away. "Damn loggerheads," Kirk muttered. He cut the buoy off, threw it forward, and elbowed the trap off the stern.

She had been watching him and forgotten to put the engine in gear.

"Let's go," he snapped, jerking his shirt off over his head.

By ten-thirty, he had pulled the first seventy-five traps—half his line.

"The tide's due to change at noon," he said, taking the wheel. "I don't think we better try pulling down tide."

Buddy knew pulling down tide meant hooking the buoy line, then backing up to the trap. She guessed he didn't think she could do it. And she was pretty sure he'd be right.

"We'll go back to the Indian Key end of the line and wait for the tide. If you're hungry," he said, rubbing his shoulders, then rotating them in circles, "get a sandwich."

Buddy sat on the cooler listening to the thunder and watching the crabs in the bin circle around, challenging each other. She had nibbled off the corner of a peanut butter and apple sandwich, decided it tasted sad, and put it back in the bag. Now, she leaned over the bin, close enough for a large boar to see her. He opened his claws, flung them wide, and backed across the rippling mass of crabs beneath him until he bumped into a corner. She smiled and wagged a finger at him, the movement of which he followed with his claws.

106

"We've got a lot of crabs, don't we?" she said, covering a yawn.

"Pretty good. About eighty pounds in claws. You tired?"

"No sir," she said and yawned again before she could stop herself. "It's gonna rain."

"We'll probably be finished before it gets here. Hand me another Coke, will you?"

She opened the lid, moved the snapper, and dug into the ice for his third Coke.

"Do you remember when you were real small, right after your grandmother died? Dad and I brought you out fishing with us, and we kept you in the fish box so we didn't have to worry about you falling overboard. You were only tall enough to see over the rim, but you'd laugh and clap every time we brought a trap up." Her father looked at her and smiled, then his expression saddened. "You were too young to remember, I guess."

"I think I do remember," she said, though she didn't and could only wish she did.

"That seems so long ago now," he said to himself.

They drifted for a quarter hour near the head of his line, waiting for the tide to change. Buddy tried to nap, but it was hot and the thunder rumbling kept her edgy. At least a breeze had kicked up. Kirk sat on the edge of the fish box eating his fourth sandwich and watching the tug of the tide around his first buoy. Minutes after noon, the flow hesitated, then resumed in the opposite direction.

They had pulled about ten traps when Buddy saw the boat about three-quarters of a mile down his line. When her father realized it had one of his traps on its stern, he pulled Buddy away from the wheel, held her arm to keep her from falling, and slapped the throttle and the gear full forward. The bow lifted out of the water, hesitated, then slammed back down and bounced full speed toward the other boat, a Mako.

Kirk pulled the power and settled in beside Jane Conroy's boat. His trap was still on the stern. "What the hell do you think you're doing," he snarled.

Jane was sitting on the gunnel with her pad in her lap, a pencil behind her ear, one of Kirk's crabs in one hand and calipers in the other. She smiled at him. "Measuring a crab." She nodded to Buddy who smiled back quickly. "From your language and the expression on your face, this must be your trapline."

Chapter 16

BUDDY GLANCED FROM MISS CONROY to her father's red and angry face.

"You're damn right, it's my trap," Kirk snapped. "What right . . ."

"I have a permit from the state to pull your traps and everyone else's. I'm doing a survey."

"What for?"

"For the Department of Natural Resources and the Park Service." She smiled broadly at him. "They are thinking about making the Park off-limits to commercial fishing."

"Bullshit."

"Perhaps, if your haul is sufficient today, you could afford a dictionary. Your vocabulary seems a bit stunted."

"My language is all that's keeping me from coming over there and pitching you overboard."

"Life's little blessings."

"You're real clever, lady, but you haven't proved to me you have any right to pull my traps."

Jane finished measuring the crab then, with an oddly shaped pair of pliers, attached a small metal tag to its carapace before putting the crab back in the trap. She pulled her backpack from the compartment under the wheel, rifled through it, came up with a piece of paper, and handed it across to Kirk.

He read it, folded it, and handed it back. "My father helped survey the Park boundaries," he said, not looking at her but at the storm, which was much nearer now. "He was at the dedication. They said it would always be open to commercial fishing."

Jane looked at him. Her face softened. "Things change."

Buddy saw that she meant it nicely, but her father didn't. His eyes narrowed.

Buddy watched Jane carefully reach in for another crab, take up the calipers and begin to measure first the claws, then the carapace.

"What exactly are you doing?" Kirk asked.

"I'm counting the number of traplines set in Park waters and spot-checking individual traps in each line."

"What are you going to find out?" Buddy said softly, then glanced up at her father.

"Hopefully, the impact of commercial crabbing on the Park's population."

"That's more bull," Kirk said calmly. "There are a zillion crabs in these waters."

"You people always think the supply is limitless." She tagged and replaced the active, angry male, then took out a soft, molting female. "There aren't nearly the number of crabs there were five years ago."

110

Kirk's eyes were on the female crab in Jane's hand.

She measured it, made a note on the pad, and dropped it over the side.

"Don't," Kirk yelled, too late. "Ah, Jesus Christ."

"That was a female," Jane said in a shame-on-you tone.

"I know that," Kirk snapped. "It was a molting female, a young honey."

"So?"

"You leave them in the trap, doctor," he sneered. "They attract big boars."

"Clearly," Jane said.

Buddy grinned and ducked her head.

"That was funny," Kirk said. "Now explain how we are reducing the numbers of stone crabs when we're only taking their claws—which grow back—and then only those of the male crabs."

"Well for one, we suspect that the claws of large females are being taken."

Buddy knew Alex's father did. He bragged about it.

"If they close the Park," Jane continued, "that will change anyway. Outside the Park boundary, you'll be allowed to take any legal-sized claw, a stupid trade-off, in my opinion, but I'm not the one making the decisions. The existing law is unenforceable anyway unless they go back to having the crabbers bring the whole crab to the docks before declawing. That practice guaranteed they all died. Now just most of them die."

"They die?" Buddy asked.

"They don't die," Kirk said to Buddy.

"Laboratory studies indicate that taking the claws kills the crab."

"Laboratory studies . . . why don't you people speak English?"

"Your level of English, Mr. Martin?" She held the female she was measuring over the side, smiled up at him. "May I?"

He made a be-my-guest motion.

"Thank you." She dropped it into the water, closed the lid of his trap, and pushed it overboard.

"Oh, and thank *you*." Kirk bowed as the heavy, crab-ladened trap sank to the bottom.

Miss Conroy nodded to Buddy and turned to start her motor.

"Ma'am," Buddy called to her. "Why does taking the claws kill them?" She looked up at her father. "I have to do a science project for school," she said. "Maybe I'll do something on stone crabs."

Jane's Mako had a hoist. She leaned over and hooked his trap again, looped the rope over the part of the hoist called the snatch block, and started the gas-powered winch. She let the hoist bring the trap up until it dangled above the stern, then she swung it in, opened the lid and, with a gloved hand, grabbed a crab. "Help yourself," she said to Kirk.

"In the lab," Jane said to Buddy, "we keep crabs in aerated tanks."

Buddy's brow wrinkled.

"Tanks with air hoses in them," she explained. "And

112

they have plenty of food. We did a test where we took one claw off a hundred crabs and both claws off another hundred. The breaking was done properly, cleanly, like this." She popped the crab's right claw off by snapping it down, sharply, at a right angle to its body. She tossed the claw to Kirk. "There was another group of a hundred, none of whose claws were taken, and none of them died."

Buddy couldn't take her eyes off Jane's face. Though her hair was dark and curly, something about her reminded Buddy of the picture of her mother. And Jane's voice was soft and deep, like she was sure her mother's had been.

"Of the crabs from which we took one claw, twenty-nine died within twenty-four hours. Of the ones that lost both claws, half died by the next day. Out here where they have to feed themselves, and defend against groupers, octopuses, conch, and other crabs with claws, we don't think any of them survive."

Buddy looked at the two bins of stone crabs, then at her father.

"That's not true," Kirk said. "I'm always finding crabs with small claws, or those nubs that grow under that sheath before they molt."

"Those have probably dropped their own claws. When a crab releases its own claw, the wound seals naturally. And it rarely loses both at the same time."

Kirk stared at her, stone-faced.

"Not only that," Jane said, peering over into the bins.

"They should be kept out of the sun and wetted down often."

"Would you like me to stop and dig clams for them, too?" Kirk sneered. "And if you're so sure they are going to die, why bother?"

"To give them a fighting chance. I'd like to see the law read that you people could only take one claw, but that's unenforceable, too. Do you know how to properly break off a claw?" she asked Kirk.

"No, I've only been doing this off and on for thirty years. Why don't you show me, doctor."

She ignored his tone and smiled at him. "I'm doing this study for my Ph.D., so I'm not a doctor yet.

"See how clean this break is," she said to Buddy. "When the claw is twisted off it tears the meat and the crab bleeds to death." She twisted off the remaining claw.

"Don't," Buddy cried, too late.

"I'm sorry," Jane said. "I wanted to show you something. See this white sticky stuff? That's the crab's blood. Put him in a bucket of water, take him home, and see how long he lives." She handed the crab to Buddy and tossed the claw to Kirk.

"I'm sorry," Buddy whispered to the crab, stroking its carapace. She pushed the snag of meat back into the break, and put her thumb over the hole. "Miss Conroy," Buddy said. "Osceola died."

"Damn," Jane muttered.

Kirk turned to Buddy. "You didn't tell me that." His brow furrowed. "Why didn't you tell me?"

114

"I guess I forgot." To Jane she said, "My grandfather and me went up to visit them, and Mr. Blossom told me Osceola died." Buddy looked down at the crab, then back at Jane. "Do you know why he died?"

"He had dolphin pox. I saw it when I was there."

"Was that the white cauliflower-looking bump near his blowhole?"

Jane nodded.

"And that little thing killed him?"

"Well, it probably wouldn't have in the wild, but the conditions Stevens has got those dolphins in are so bad it probably weakened him and left him open to some other infection."

"Will the others get it?"

Jane's lips were compressed to a fine line. "I don't know," she said finally.

Buddy bit at the corner of her lip.

Jane glanced at Kirk, then back at Buddy. "I don't think they will, honey. He's learned his lesson. He'll take better care of the other two."

Buddy studied Jane's face and saw kindness, maybe even pity, and she knew that Miss Conroy was only hoping, too. She nodded sadly, and stroked the crab.

"Look," Jane said, reaching to touch Buddy's hand. "Why don't you come by after school one day and I'll help you with your science project. I'm staying in cabin nine at the Rod and Gun Club."

Buddy glanced at her father, who nodded. "I'm not sure if I can really do stone crabs," she said to Jane.

"Alex Townsend told Miss Daniels he wanted to do them."

"Ruth Daniels is a friend of mine," Jane said. "I'll ask her to let you do them, if you want me to."

Buddy's head bobbed. "Oh yes, please."

"How about Monday at three-thirty, okay?"

"Sure." She smiled.

Nearer now, the thunder rumbled.

Chapter 17

BUDDY HELD THE CRAB IN ONE HAND, with her thumb over the hole in its side, and steered with the other. When they idled for Kirk to pull a trap, she held the crab underwater so it wouldn't dry out. Its legs moved in search of freedom.

Kirk missed a trap because she had veered off course. "Damn it, Buddy, throw that thing overboard and pay attention to what you're doing."

"He'll die."

"Then put him in the bucket until we get through."

In her mind she saw the blood from the Admiral's shoulder swirling around them in the river. "Please, Daddy, he'll bleed to death."

The first raindrop stung her cheek. A black wall of clouds moved toward them from the south.

"Okay," her father snapped. He reached passed her and jerked the wheel hard to the right, jammed it in reverse, and roared backward toward his buoy. "You nurse the crab, I'll finish alone." He spun her by the shoulder and pushed her toward the cabin.

Kirk grabbed the broom handle and reached over the stern. "Damn it," he snarled. He'd backed over the buoy and wrapped the line around the prop. He glanced at her as if it were her fault, stripped to his underwear, ripped his gloves off, threw them down, and dove overboard.

Buddy carried the bucket of saltwater into the trunk cabin, crawled up on a pile of nets, and sat with her knees pulled up to her chest. "I've done it now," she told the crab, lowering him into the bucket.

Kirk came up, expelled air, sucked in another lungful, and went down again. Thunder boomed closer. Rain pelted the choppy surface of the bay. The wind turned cold and frantic.

When he got back in the boat and pulled the trap, it was empty, its galvanized core and one side were missing, probably broken out by a loggerhead. "Damn turtles," he hissed, swinging the trap aboard. It hit the deck at the exact moment thunder crashed over them. Buddy released the crab, rolled in a ball, and plugged her ears.

When her father put the engine in gear, Buddy peeked up. Rivulets of water ran from his matted black curls down his face and chest. He squinted against the sting of the wind-driven rain and watched for his next trap.

She was cold and trembled from it. An old, torn, dried-hard towel was in the opposite corner of the cabin. She stretched a long, chill-bump-covered leg out, hooked a corner with her big toe, and dragged it over. Two roaches fell out when she shook and smoothed it. One scurried into the net and the other ran up the leg of her shorts. She shuddered and squashed it, wiped her hip with the towel, and threw it back in the corner. Buddy reached in the bucket, caught the scuttling crab, and put her thumb back over its wound.

There was a searing light and the thunder was explosive. Kirk threw his arm over his head and ducked.

"Daddy!" she screamed and started violently, knocking the bucket over. She curled into a ball and rolled on her side, pressed her forearms to her ears and plugged her eyes with her kneecaps. "Daddy," she cried, "Daddy, please, I'm scared."

Kirk put the engine in reverse and backed slowly toward the buoy he had missed. "It's all right, Buddy. It's gone now."

But she stayed rolled in a tight ball with her arms wrapped around her head until a warmth touched her shoulder. It was the sun, but to her it was the Admiral's hand. She clutched her shirt where it was warm and listened as the distant rumble of the departing storm became her grandfather's deep and soothing voice.

Within the hour, the stillness of the morning returned. Buddy found the crab lodged in the port scupper. She dipped the bucket, put the crab in, crawled back up in the net, and silently watched her father.

"Is there still Coke in the cooler?" he asked.

"Yes, sir. I think so." She let go of the crab and jumped up to get him a drink.

119

"Three more and we're through. You want to take us in?"

She side-eyed the bucket, but said: "Yes, sir."

"That was quite a storm." He patted her shoulder, drained the Coke in one long swallow, and tossed the bottle overboard. It righted itself and bobbed away in water nearly the same color as the bottle.

"There should be a buoy here," Kirk said to himself. He looked ahead to the next trap, then back at the last one. "Damn tourists." He gunned it and went on.

"Why damn tourists?" Buddy asked.

"They run over our lines, but instead of taking the time to get untangled, they cut themselves loose and we lose a trap."

"Are the crabs trapped in there forever then?"

"We are certainly into worrying about crabs all of a sudden, aren't we?"

Buddy lowered her eyes.

"The trap rots away, okay? But let me tell you something. Bleeding hearts are always coming along wailing about killing crabs, shooting deer, feeding a bad fish to a dolphin, but they've got nothing at stake. They make their livings in offices somewhere, and they don't have to kill what they order up in a restaurant or buy packaged and bloodless in a grocery store. It's easy for them to care about things they don't *have* to care about. Do you understand?" His face was so close, she could smell the Coke on his breath. "I do care about the crabs and the deer and the lobsters and the fish." He ticked them off on his fingers.

120

"All of them, because they feed us. That's why I don't take the females even though, in a fish basket on the scales, the Feds can't tell female claws from male. I don't take them because they are protected and I believe they should be. So don't belly up to a plate of crab claws tonight and give me this conservation crap now. Got it?"

She was leaning so far back, her stomach muscles quivered. She nodded.

Buddy tried to watch him declawing without looking as if she was watching. Done right, it made a snapping sound she soon became comfortable with. Snap, snap, she'd hear, then see the splash she couldn't hear over the engine. Snap, snap, splash. For an hour and a half, crab after crab somersaulted through the air and disappeared in the foam of their wake. Twice, when he muttered damn, she looked in time to see the claws disappear over the side and the crab land in the claw bin.

At the dock, there was a line at the fish house waiting to have their catch weighed. Crabbers lolled on decks, drinking Budweisers, smoking, and complaining about how lousy their hauls were. Buddy had never heard a fisherman admit to a good day. The Admiral said it was so other fishermen wouldn't move their lines near yours. He told her about the time he brought in so many claws that the next time he went to pull his line, he couldn't find it in the crowd.

Her father never joined in these discussions. He exchanged nods as he guided his boat in, but that was all.

No one offered him a beer or asked about his day, except Carlisle Townsend. He was the only one who always ignored Kirk's coolness. And it apparently didn't bother him that Kirk rarely responded. Like his son, Townsend was a braggart. To him a quiet audience was engaged.

"Looks like you got a nice haul there, Martin," Townsend called from the dock. "Considering the number of traps you got out."

Kirk nodded and continued washing down the deck with the hose from the dock.

"I hauled nearly seven hundred pounds."

"How many of them were females?" Kirk muttered.

"About half." Carlisle laughed. "Not really. A third, maybe. From the barnacles, I'd say most of 'em were locals this time. We get a good nor'wester, and them suckers start walking, I bet I double my haul."

"I'll pray for you," Kirk said, under his breath.

Buddy put her bucket on the dock and hoisted herself up beside it.

"Whatcha got there, Buddy?" Alex's father asked.

"A stone crab."

"It's against the law to keep a crab." He grinned at Kirk and winked.

"Miss Conroy gave him to me."

"Who's she?" he asked Kirk.

"Just some broad out there counting crabs."

"What's she counting crabs for?"

Kirk shrugged, then his face got a friendly look. He gave Buddy a conspiratorial glance and folded the hose in half to stop the water. "She said she was checking on the ratio of females to males in the traps so the Park people can get an idea how many females are being taken illegally."

Buddy was standing on the dock a little behind Mr. Townsend. She grinned down at her father, then peeked around to see Carlisle's usual puffed-up, self-important expression deflate like someone had stuck a pin in his cheek. She smiled up at Alex's father. "She's real nice, Mr. Townsend. She gave me this crab for my science project."

"She was working my traps today," Kirk said. "I can't remember whether she said she had already checked yours or not." Kirk scratched his head, as if trying to remember, then shrugged, and let the water through the hose again.

Townsend spun and walked down the dock.

Kirk glanced up and winked at her. Buddy laughed, scooped up her bucket, and skipped down the road toward home. She stopped once to look back. Alex's father was with a knot of other crabbers. Smoke from their cigarettes rose out of their tight circle so they looked like a pile of leaves before the fire catches.

Chapter 18

WHEN HER FATHER CAME INTO THE KITCHEN, Buddy had just finished telling the Admiral about their meeting with Jane and the joke on Carlisle Townsend. They were sitting at the kitchen table, laughing, with the crab between them. Buddy was trying to get it to eat the small squares of bacon she had cut.

"It's not going to eat bacon, especially not sitting on the table." Kirk washed his hands then filled a pot with water. "Why don't you let it go down by Smallwood's."

"If he doesn't die, I can use him in my science project."

"Oh yeah. I forgot about that." He put the pot on a burner and dumped a bag of claws into the sink. "I got $900 for three hundred pounds. At that measly price we might as well eat them ourselves."

Buddy swiveled in her chair. "What do crabs eat?" she whispered to the Admiral, scraping the bacon bits off into a napkin.

"Clams and oysters, mostly. You named him yet?"

She thought for a minute. "Maybe I could name him Osceola. Do you think that's bad luck, Admiral?"

"No. He's a lucky crab to have you take care of him and that dolphin would like having a tough little namesake to be remembered by."

"Good." She smacked her thigh. "His name is Osceola."

"You know, we used to have a fish tank. I ain't seen it in years, but your grandma never gave nothing away so it must be here somewhere."

"It's under the front porch," Kirk said. "I saw it there a few months ago."

Buddy put Osceola in the bucket and darted out the door, letting it bang shut behind her. "Sorry," she shouted. Minutes later, she came in with the fish tank under her arm. She had washed it at the dock, but not the sand off her knees or elbows, and she had a cobweb in her hair.

". . . you really think they're going to close the Park?" the Admiral was asking.

"I don't know." Steam rose from the pot. "Buddy, look what you're doing," Kirk said, pointing to the puddle forming on the floor.

"Sorry." Buddy grabbed the dish towel off the refrigerator handle, wiped the fish tank, then the floor.

"I bet they do close it," the Admiral said. "A promise made by the government is as useless as the politician that makes it. Remember old man Smallwood's 167 acres. He helped them survey it, then they took it for his trouble. Yep, they'll close it," he said.

"Damn it, Buddy, that's a clean dish towel." Kirk snatched it out of her hand.

"I'm sorry."

"Quit saying, I'm sorry. Just think about what the hell you're doing and you won't have to be sorry."

"Quit yelling at her," the Admiral shouted.

"Mind your own business," Kirk snapped.

Buddy took the bucket and the tank and backed out the door.

"She takes enough of a beating without you yelling at her. And she's as much my business as she is yours."

Buddy sat down on the top step beneath the kitchen window.

"She needs to pay attention to what she's doing."

"It's a little water on the floor."

"Look, I've had a brutal day so get off my back," Kirk snapped.

"Son, you've got your priorities all screwed up. But someday you're gonna realize what you've lost." He hesitated then shouted, "I wish that on you."

When Buddy heard her grandfather bash through the door to the living room, she got up. Osceola scuttled around and around his plastic prison. "I know how you feel," she whispered, "but as soon as you're well, I'll let you go. I promise." She hiked the tank up on her hip and headed down the road, through the pines, to Smallwood's store.

Years ago, Ted Smallwood had cleared away some red mangroves and sea grapes to expose a narrow strip of sand as a place for the Indians to land their canoes.

Buddy set the bucket on the seawall and waded out from this beach with the aquarium past where small waves rolled over on themselves. In cupped hands, she scooped sand into the tank until it was about two inches deep. Then it suddenly listed and sank to the bottom. She emptied it and brought it to the seawall. "This ain't gonna work," she told the crab. "I'll be back, okay?" She started off at a run, stopped, came back, carried the tank and the bucket to the bushes by the old boat cradle, then ran off through the pines.

"Admiral?" she tapped on his door.

There was no answer.

"Admiral?" She rapped louder and opened the door a crack.

He opened his eyes. "Hi, honey."

"Admiral, Osceola's tank is gonna be too heavy for me to carry back."

"Where's your father?"

"I don't know. In the kitchen still, maybe. I don't want to ask him, Admiral. He's mad at me and don't like the crab none either."

He stroked her arm. "How about the wheelbarrow?"

"The wheel's off, remember?"

"Oh, yeah."

"Admiral, can I borrow your wheelchair? I'll be careful and I wouldn't get it wet."

"I ain't worried about you getting it wet. Wet dries. Ain't you smart to think of it."

She kissed his stubbly cheek. "Thanks."

When she got the chair off the porch, she kicked up the footrests, got in, launched off with her bare feet and spun the wheels as hard as she could. The trail from her house through the pines was slightly downhill. When she was flying, she threw her legs out straight, flung her arms wide, and tilted her head up into the wind.

Before she wheeled the tank back, she put Osceola in it and watched as he bashed himself into first one side, then the other. She scooped up a half bucket of water, put it in the seat with the tank, then waded into the shallows and walked back and forth digging her toes into the sand for clams. When she had gotten half a dozen, she marched her collection home.

Buddy parked the chair at the bottom of the ramp, tiptoed up, quietly opened the screen door, and peeked in. The kitchen was empty. She carried the bucket up first and used it to prop open the door. Once inside with the tank, she reloaded the bucket. The shower was running as she wheeled passed the bathroom into her bedroom.

Buddy cleared a spot on her dresser, then put the tank against the mirror so Osceola could keep himself company. His tracks pocked the sand as he scurried back and forth, bumping the glass, north, south, east, and west. "You need to hide, don't you? I'll get you something. Wait here."

She felt the need to sneak about, to keep attention away from herself and the crab, so she tiptoed past the bathroom where she could hear the shower dripping and the scrape of a razor across a cheek.

In the shed, she chose the oldest trap, broke the tubular, steel bait chute loose, then dragged the trap to the darkest corner and stacked two other traps on top of it.

She stood on the front porch, listening, before she quietly opened the screen door and slid in through the crack. She had stuck the metal tube in the waistband of her shorts, behind her back, and pulled her T-shirt over the top of it. She crept across the living room, past her father's bedroom door. Her hand was on her doorknob when he touched her shoulder.

"You ready for dinner?"

She spun and pressed her back against her door.

"Are you still messing with that crab?"

"No, sir. Well, yes, sir."

"Well get done and clean up for dinner."

"Yes, sir." She backed into her room.

Osceola had partially buried himself in the sand. She smiled at him over the rim. "I can see you."

Puffs of sand exploded into the shallow layer of water.

"That did it, you're gone now." Buddy put the tube in the tank, added most of the water, and dropped all the clams in except one which she left in the bucket. "I'll open this one for you after dinner," she said, holding the bucket up for him to see. "Bye." She waved, and took the wheelchair with her.

Her grandfather was snoring, softly, when she parked his chair beside his bed. "Thanks, Admiral," she whispered.

At dinner Buddy pushed the claws to one side of her plate and ate her string beans and potatoes.

"Why aren't you eating the claws?"

"I will. I'm saving them."

When he wasn't looking, she turned each claw so she could see if the broken end was ragged. None were. She felt better.

After she did the dishes, Buddy got a sharp knife, turned the clam on its flattest side, worked the blade between the two shell halves, and pushed down as hard as she could. The blade went through the clam and the bucket. Water seeped slowly out of the crack in the plastic. Buddy grabbed the bucket, put her hand under the puncture, and ran from her room toward the porch. She hit her father as he came out of the bathroom. Some water splashed up the side and soaked the front of his shirt, the rest dripped out on his shoes.

"I can't believe this," Kirk said calmly. "What are you doing?" His voice more strained.

"I was trying to open a clam for Osceola," she whispered.

He seemed to try, for a moment, not to yell. "You know better than to play with a knife. Don't you?" His fists knotted and unknotted.

"I wasn't playing." The bucket was empty now. They were standing in the puddle.

"Screwing with that stone crab is playing." He was yelling now.

She hung her head.

"And you've ruined that bucket. They're expensive and I

have to get them in Naples." He snatched it away from her, stomped across the living room, opened the screen door, and sailed it off the porch, clam and all. "Now clean up this mess."

A tear rolled down her cheek and splashed into the puddle at her feet.

"And don't cry." He shook his finger at her. "It's about time you grew up," he shouted, stomped into his room and slammed the door. "And get rid of that crab," he yelled.

Osceola was out of his tube when she came into the room and flung herself across her bed. He shot into it and clunked against the glass at the other end.

It was morning, but still dark, when Buddy heard her door open. She didn't turn or open her eyes, but she held her breath as the floor creaked under her father's weight. He stopped at the end of her bed and just stood there for what seemed like a long time. She could hear him breathing.

Her right foot was out from under the sheet. She felt her father gently lift it, pull the sheet free, cover her and tuck in the corner, then she heard the boards creak as he walked away. "I'm sorry, honey," he whispered, just before he closed the door.

"Me, too," she whispered back.

Chapter 19

WHEN BUDDY WOKE AGAIN, the sky was graying. She dug a clam out of the sand in the tank, crept out of her room and into the kitchen. She jumped up on locked arms and looked out the kitchen window. Her father's boat was gone.

She went outside and smashed the clam with a coconut, then took the flat blob to the kitchen sink to rinse the sand and shell bits off. Carefully, she sliced the clam into tiny pieces.

Back in her room, Buddy tapped on the glass and dropped a piece of clam into the water. It settled on top of the tube. The next one drifted down and came to rest just at the opening. She sat on the edge of her bed and waited.

The tip of a jointed leg appeared, then half a crab. A tiny pincer opened, reached slowly out, picked up the piece of clam, and carried it to his mouth. Two flat flaps opened up and the clam was sucked in.

Buddy dumped the rest of the chunks into the tank,

took her cap from the bedpost, peeked in on her sleeping grandfather, then left the house.

Near the trash pile at the end of the Stevens's levee, Buddy cut the pitpan's motor and let it drift into some cattails. It was early and there were no tourists yet, but it was still too open to walk from there to the pond, so she poled along the bank and tied up tight into the willows.

On the far side of the pond, near the gate to the show pool, both dolphins surfaced, expelled air, and disappeared. Buddy straddled the pipe and patted the surface of the water, her eyes locked on the spot where they had gone under. The warm, scummy feel of the water on her palm suddenly became cool and slick. She looked down to see that she was touching the face of a dolphin, right behind its eye. Surprise caused her to jerk her hand back. The dolphin zipped away.

"Annie? Lucie? I'm sorry, you scared me," Buddy said. "Please come back."

The dolphin with the pink scar on her snout cruised past on its side, apparently grinning.

"Hi, Annie." Buddy smiled and waved. "It's me. Buddy Martin."

The dolphin circled, drew up at the end of the culvert, stood on her tail, squeaked and tossed her head.

Buddy smiled, bent low over the pipe and extended her hand slowly, palm up, but she did not try to touch Annie. They looked at each other for a moment, then Annie lowered her head and laid her snout in Buddy's palm.

133

Buddy felt a rush of heat from the tip of her toes dangling in the water to the top of her head. Her heart pounded as she slowly, carefully, covered the dolphin's snout with her other hand, leaned over and kissed its scarred tip, then cautiously put her arms around the dolphin's thick neck. When the dolphin didn't move away, Buddy pressed her cheek to Annie's and closed her eyes.

It was the sudden, unexpected clatter of the metal folding doors on the gift shop opening that startled Annie. In an instant the dolphin was gone from the circle of Buddy's arms, leaving her suspended for a moment over the water before she toppled in head first.

Nearly the instant she hit the water, she was lifted out again, draped like wet moss across Annie's snout and forehead. Buddy screamed, flung herself sideways, and went under, sucked deep beneath the surface in the eddy of the dolphin's departure. With no air in her lungs, she fought her way up toward the murky light and burst out of the water, gasping. She spun, looking for the dolphin.

Annie was near the gate to the show pool.

"I'm sorry," Buddy choked. "I know you wouldn't hurt me." She put her hand out and Annie came slowly toward her, stopped and turned on her side to expose her smile before she sank away and swam a circle around her. Buddy felt her pass, felt the pressure the movement of her tail made in the water. She turned, trying to keep track of where the dolphin was. Suddenly, Annie's dorsal fin arched up behind her and slid into her hand. Buddy caught it at the narrow tip, then quickly let go, afraid she was too heavy.

Annie dove, circled, and came up again. Her fin slid against Buddy's palm, which closed low over the broadest part. Annie gave a pump of her tail, dragging Buddy toward the cattails at the far end of the pond. In front of the cattails, she swirled to the right. Buddy rolled off laughing and bumped to a stop, sitting shoulder deep in the shallow water.

"Oh, Annie," she said, when the dolphin nosed in next to her and nudged her head onto Buddy's lap, "that was wonderful." Buddy put her arms across Annie's back, one on either side of her blowhole and kissed her: "Smack, smack, smack."

Annie jerked her head up and brought it down heavily, splashing Buddy and rocking her, then raised it up again, flopped sideways and zipped across the pond. When she came back, a sea grape leaf was stuck to her forehead. Buddy plucked it off and flicked the tip of Annie's snout with it. Annie snatched it, twisted, and skimmed away.

"Give me that leaf." Buddy leapt after her.

Annie released it and upended.

Buddy swam slowly, sneakylike, as if Annie couldn't tell she was moving. Inches from where the leaf bobbed between them, Buddy's hand shot out. Annie, in a blink, snatched it and dove, popping up a second later just behind her.

Buddy whirled and lunged at her.

Annie flopped sideways.

Buddy remembered Stevens's son saying Annie liked having her tongue tickled. "If you give me the leaf, I'll tickle your tongue," Buddy said, wiggling her fingers in the air.

Annie opened her mouth and let the leaf float out.

Buddy ran one finger along Annie's lower row of teeth then danced her fingers up and down the pink tongue. The leaf bobbed in the water beside them. Buddy grinned suddenly. "It's mine now," she cried, snatched it, splashed the dolphin, and dove under.

She felt the suction as Annie passed beneath her. Buddy let herself bob to the surface, took a breath, then dangled face down, making a slow circle, trying to find the dolphin. From directly beneath her, Annie loomed up out of the murky water. That monstrous form moving slowly toward her flooded Buddy with the same fear she'd felt when she first fell into the water. Panic welled in her chest, flattening her lungs against her ribs until her breath left her in a gasp. But she did not move nor did she scream, and in that moment she realized that her fear had exploded on the surface in that bubble of her air. The emptiness in her chest suddenly filled with love for this smile coming toward her through the muddy water. Buddy reached down and touched the side of Annie's face before lifting her head to refill her lungs with air.

The dolphin had stopped, leaving her cheek against her palm until the moment Buddy lifted her head, then Annie pumped herself high out of the water and spun in a circle, splashing Buddy with her flippers. Buddy twirled with her arms outstretched and splashed Annie.

"I'll race you," she challenged, diving away from the dolphin.

Annie flashed by her, covering Buddy with her wake, then made a tight circle and gently brought her dorsal fin into Buddy's hand.

"Buddy Martin!" Stevens bellowed. "Get out of there!"

Alex stood on the levee between his uncle and an Ochopee policeman. He grinned, tilted back on his heels, glanced quickly from one to the other, then stuck his tongue out at her.

Buddy swam slowly back to the culvert, swinging one leaden arm after the other, barely kicking her feet. She wanted to sink into the cloudy water like Annie had done, quit lifting her heavy arms and disappear, drift to the bottom and wait for them to go away.

The policeman stepped down onto the culvert and reached his hand out to her. She treaded water and looked up at him before taking it, putting her foot on the edge of the pipe and letting herself be pulled out and up beside him.

"Hi, Dumb Buddy," Alex said, his grin nearly splitting his face.

"Go back to the booth," Stevens ordered, smacking the back of Alex's head.

"Aw, come on. I'm the one what . . ."

"Git." His uncle shoved him. When Alex moved only a few feet, Stevens stomped the ground and pointed down the levee.

Alex ran a few yards, stopped, turned, stuck his tongue out and his thumbs in his ears and waved his hands back and forth.

"Son," the policeman said, "you . . ."

"I ain't a boy," Buddy said, staring down the levee at Alex.

"Oh. They called you Buddy."

She turned to the policeman. "That's my name. Buddy Martin, but I ain't a boy. They call him Orange Blossom," she added, looking at Stevens, "but he ain't."

The cop grinned, covered his mouth and coughed.

"Watch your mouth, girlie," Stevens growled. To the cop, he said: "I want you to take her to jail. This here's the second time she's been here teasing my dolphins."

Buddy's eyes widened. "I ain't teasing the dolphins," she said to the cop, touching his hand. "Annie and me are friends. We were playing."

Stevens snorted. "My taxes pay your salary." He poked the cop in the shoulder. "Arrest her," he ordered and stomped away.

In the water, an eye and a gray cheek broke the surface.

The cop, head shaking, lips tight, turned from watching Stevens's departure and brushed off his shoulder.

"Are you going to arrest me?"

"No," he said, smiling down at her. "And I don't believe you're teasing the dolphins. I think you believe they are your friends, but . . . ," he put a hand on her shoulder and lifted her chin with the other, ". . . they belong to Mr. . . . , old Orange Blossom," he said grinning. "You can't swim with them. Besides, it could be dangerous."

"It ain't," she said softly, moving her face free of his hand and looking down at her toes curling and uncurling in the wet sand and shells. "Annie wouldn't hurt me."

In the water, beside the drain pipe, Annie squeaked and shook her head from side to side.

"Well, I'll be dipped," he said, and grinned in surprise before he could help himself. He looked away quickly and cleared his throat. "I'm sorry," he said. "You still can't come here anymore. If you do, I'll have to call your parents."

"I 'spect my dad knows where I am and my ma's right here." She tapped her chest.

A confused look rippled across the policeman's face, then sadness filled it. He glanced away. "That's where my mother is, too," he said softly. He straightened his shoulders, took her hand, and patted it. "I'm sorry, honey, you're trespassing. It's against the law to trespass."

Annie made clicking sounds behind her. When Buddy turned, Annie lifted out of the water, head bobbing, then flopped backward into the pond with a grand splash.

Buddy turned back to the policeman. "It ain't right. She's my friend. She wants to see me."

"It's not up to her—or you. They belong to him. He can do as he pleases with them."

"It used to be okay to own colored people."

"That was different," he said. "Somehow," he added, before he took her hand and started walking down the levee. Annie moved along in the water beside them. "Did you ride your bike here?"

"No, sir. I came up the river."

"Where's your boat?"

"In the willows." Buddy pointed behind them.

139

"Oh." He turned, exchanged the hand he was holding, and retraced their steps. Annie turned and swam back beside them. Off the end of the culvert, she lifted up, squealed, then twirled, spraying an arc of water.

"I can't, Annie," Buddy said. "They won't let me."

The dolphin disappeared.

"I'm sorry," the policeman said. "Really sorry."

From the pond came a series of whistles and clicks. Annie flopped over sideways, swam in a tight circle, then popped up in the center of the eddy she'd made. She bounced her head, squeaked, and let her jaw drop. On her tongue was the tattered, shredded sea grape leaf.

"Oh, Annie," Buddy cried, jerked her hand free of the policeman's, jumped down, waded into the pond, and sat down in the water. Annie propelled herself up and put her head across Buddy's thighs.

"Young lady," the policeman said.

Buddy turned and looked up at him.

"When I was your age," he said, "I'd have given anything to have a friend like Annie. So when you come back to see her . . . ," he winked, ". . . don't get caught." He bowed, tipped his hat, and walked away whistling softly.

Chapter 20

THE FOLLOWING MONDAY AFTERNOON, Buddy walked the seawall from school to the Rod and Gun Club, past cabin nine. She slipped quietly into the dark, pecky cypress-paneled lobby of the hotel, took a chair opposite the grandfather clock, and watched the hand flick from minute to minute. At three-thirty, she got up, walked down the steps, across the lawn and back along the seawall to Miss Conroy's cabin. She rapped shyly on the screen door.

"Come in, Buddy," Jane called.

It was dim in the cabin and very bright outside. Buddy closed the screen door softly behind her and stood still while her eyes adjusted.

"Hello." Jane stuck her head out of the little kitchen. "I'm fixing us a snack. Make yourself comfortable."

"Yes, ma'am." Buddy looked around then took the stiff-backed chair near the door.

Miss Conroy came out of the kitchen carrying a plate of

Oreos. "I said make yourself comfortable," she said, and smiled. "That chair belonged to the Marquis de Sade."

"Ma'am?"

"The first guy to make kids eat spinach."

Buddy laughed and leaped up.

Jane put the cookies on the coffee table in front of the sofa, went back to the kitchen, and returned with two glasses and a bottle of milk hugged to her chest. "Help yourself."

Kirk never bought cookies. Buddy took three, thought perhaps that was too many, and put one back.

"I heard about your grandfather's accident. How's he feeling?"

"About the same. I'll be glad when his shoulder's better. He's my best friend, and I miss us doing stuff together," Buddy said.

"Tell me about your other friends," Jane said, taking a cookie.

"Well, ma'am," Buddy said, without self-pity, "I ain't really got another friend, but if I did, the Admiral would still be my best one."

"I didn't have friends when I was your age, either, and no grandfather to make up for them."

Buddy was surprised. "Why didn't you have friends?"

"I was an army brat. We never lived anywhere long enough for me to make a friend, or if I did, to keep one."

Buddy had no idea what an army brat was, but it didn't sound like something Miss Conroy would like to have to explain. However, she thought she should probably indicate she felt bad about it. "That's a shame, ma'am."

"Ma'am is a little formal, don't you think? My name's Jane. Okay?"

"Yes ma' . . . sorry, Jane." She hesitated. "Jane's a nice name for a lady. Buddy don't sound like a girl's name, does it?"

"Buddy's a nice name, too. It sounds like you're a friend before anyone even knows you."

"I never thought of that."

"What's your real name?"

"Elizabeth."

"Would you rather be called Elizabeth?"

"I don't guess nobody would know who I was then."

"Would you like me to call you Elizabeth?"

"I don't know. I think it's too fancy a name for me."

"People grow into their names. Grow until they fit just right. My father used to call me Janie, but it doesn't suit me anymore."

Buddy smiled. "Elizabeth," she said softly, then grinned. "The Admiral's name fits him real good." She nodded in agreement with her own statement. "Yep, it's perfect for him," she said, then a sly grin crept across her face. "What do you think about my dad's name?"

But to Buddy's disappointment, Jane shrugged and said, "It's hard to say, isn't it? I guess it fits him. How's your crab?"

"He's fine. I named him Osceola after Mr. Blossom's dolphin."

Jane laughed. "Mr. Blossom?"

"Dad told me Mr. Stevens's friends call him Orange Blossom."

Jane whooped and slapped her thigh. "Now that's a perfect name for that blowhard."

Buddy laughed, too, then waited for Jane to stop laughing before she asked, "What's a blowhard?"

"A braggart. Somebody that's always talking and never saying anything. You know what I mean?"

"Boy, do I. I got one of them baggarts in my class at school. He's Mr. Blossom's nephew."

Jane rocked back in her chair laughing but didn't correct Buddy. "That's another strike for nature over nurture."

"Ma'am?"

"Scientists have been arguing for years about whether we humans are shaped, you know, our personalities, by what we inherit from our parents—nature, or by the way we are raised—nurture."

"Oh." Buddy nodded. "If you're interested," she said, leaning nearer. "Alex didn't get his uncle's lip."

Jane burst out laughing. "Life's not fair, is it?"

Buddy grinned. "No, it ain't. The Admiral told me there was a boy once whose nose grew every time he told a lie."

"Pinocchio."

"That's him. Well, when Alex teases me 'cause I can't read too good," Buddy glanced toward the door and lowered her voice, "I wish Mr. Blossom's lip on him. I shouldn't, I guess, but it ain't worked yet anyway." She sat back and shrugged. "Maybe teasing ain't considered as bad as lying."

"It should be. Keep wishing." Jane snapped her fingers.

144

"I forgot to tell you, I talked to Miss Daniels yesterday about your report."

"Yes ma'am . . . sorry, Jane, she told me. Thank you."

"Well I thought maybe you'd like to go out with me one day, and I'll show you how I do my research and what I'm learning. Would you like that?"

"Oh yes ma' . . . , yes, I would, but . . .," she dropped her eyes for a second and bit her lip. "I ain't much help. You sure you want me to go?"

"Of course. I'm not asking you because I need help, I'm asking you because I'd like you to come. I get lonesome out there working by myself. And what makes you think you aren't much help?"

"I get things like directions confused. They seem right to me and the Admiral, but to other people they ain't right. They're backwardlike."

"Is that why you have trouble reading?"

"And doing arithmetic and steering a boat . . ." She stood up and walked to the mirror mounted on the outside of the door to the bathroom. "For me, the only time things is the way they should be is in a mirror."

"What do you mean?" Jane's eyes narrowed. "Explain that to me." She walked over and stood behind Buddy.

"I don't make mistakes in the mirror." Buddy slung her arms out to the right then swung them left, raised them in an arc over her head, spun herself on tiptoes, caught Jane's eye, blushed, and put her arms down.

Jane stared at their reflections, turned, grabbed a magazine off the coffee table and held it up to the mirror. "It's not just backward," she said, "it's reversed." A huge smile bloomed. "Reversed." She laughed, and grabbed Buddy by the shoulders. "How would you like to go to Miami?"

"To Miami?"

"To Miami."

"Oh, yes, ma'am. I'd love to go to Miami."

"I want to ask Ruth Daniels something, then I'll call and ask your father. Okay?"

Buddy's heart sank. "We ain't got a phone."

"That's okay. I'm in Chokoloskee two or three times a week. I'll stop by and ask him next time I'm there."

Chapter 21

BUDDY STOOD IN THE DOORWAY of her grandfather's room watching his chest rise and fall. He was propped up in bed with three pillows behind his head. The room smelled stuffy and stale. His lunch, an untouched sandwich, was on his bedside table.

"Admiral, are you asleep?" Buddy whispered.

"Nupe." He drew his lips tight across his gums in a grin.

She pulled his wheelchair around and sat down. "How come you're sitting here in bed with the blinds closed and the light on?"

"I don't know. There wasn't nothing to do, and I got tired of sitting on the porch."

"You're okay, ain't you?"

"Sure I'm okay, honey. I'm just lazy today. Whatcha up to?"

She watched his face for a moment, then nodded. "I been visiting that biology lady. Remember? Miss Conroy. Her name is Jane."

"I remember."

"Don't tell Dad this yet. Okay?" She lowered her voice. "I told Jane about things being right for me—for us—in mirrors and, for some reason, she got all excited and asked me to go to Miami." Buddy clapped her hands together.

"Well," he said, blinked and glanced away.

"Admiral?" She took his hand and worked the wrinkles down toward the tips of his fingers.

He looked back at her and smiled. "That's real nice, honey."

Buddy's brow creased. "You know, before she asked me to go, I was telling her about you being my best friend."

He patted her hand then leaned his head back on the pillows and closed his eyes. She didn't like the color of his skin in the lamplight. "Do you want me to open the blinds and turn out the light?"

"No, I want the light on." His eyes were still closed.

Buddy sighed and stood up. "I guess I'll feed Osceola." She stopped at the door. "I miss you, Admiral. Promise you'll feel better soon."

"I promise to try, honey," he said, opening his eyes, then shielding them against the afternoon sun behind her. "You looked so tall there in the light, getting all growed up."

She bit her lip. "I ain't though."

Kirk was in the shower when Buddy filched a hammer from the shed and smashed a clam on the front porch step.

"Whatcha doing?" he asked, his hair slicked back and wet.

At the sound of her father's voice, Buddy started. "I'll clean it up," she gasped, edging the hammer off the step into the bushes with the side of her hand.

"That's okay," Kirk said. "How's he doing?"

"Who?"

"Your crab."

"Osceola?" she asked, then answered, "He's fine."

"That's good. How was school today?"

"Fine, thank you."

"And your meeting with Miss Conroy?"

"Fine."

"That's nice." He smiled. "I thought I'd barbecue some lobster for dinner. Does that sound good?"

She loved lobster. "Yes, sir."

"I'll barbecue some corn on the cob, too. Would you like that?"

She loved corn on the cob. "Yes, sir."

"Well, good. That's settled." He jammed his hands in his pockets and looked past her toward the docks. "Well then," he said finally, "guess I'll see you later." But he didn't move. He nodded toward the wad of smashed clam on the step. "He likes that, huh?"

"Yes, sir."

He squeezed his lips together. "I like clams, too. Guess we crabs have the same tastes." He patted her shoulder and walked away, leaving her to wonder if that was some kind of apology.

~ ~ ~

Three days later, through the dirty school bus window, Buddy watched Jane's Volkswagen pull away from the stop sign at the top of the hill above her house and turn right, headed back toward Everglades City.

She could also see that her father's truck was backed up to the shed. The instant the bus driver opened the door, Buddy leapt down and raced across the yard. Kirk was unloading cans of paint. "Was Jane here?" she asked, grinning.

"Don't you think you should call her Miss Conroy?"

"She told me to call her Jane. Did she ask you if I could go to Miami with her?"

"Yes."

"Can I go?"

"May I."

"May I?"

He looked at her, then smiled. "Yes."

Buddy grinned, broadly, ran to the truck, grabbed two cans of paint, brought them to him, then ran to get two more.

When he finished stacking all the cans, he unrolled a large piece of plastic, cut a sheet, and covered the cans with it.

"Whatcha gonna do with that paint?"

"Paint the house, when it's cooler."

"Can I . . . may I help?"

"Maybe," he said, bending over to tuck a corner of the plastic under a paint can.

"Did Jane tell you why she asked me to go to Miami?"

"Well, she talked about mirrors, and seeing things in reverse, and whether I had ever had problems reading? Nothing that seemed to make any more sense than she usually does."

"Why did you say yes then?"

"Because she seemed so positive that the problems you have reading can be fixed. The doctor she wants you to see is there."

"A doctor?"

"She specializes in learning disabilities."

"Oh." Buddy worked her toes into the grass. That confused her a little. They said the Admiral was disabled, and it wasn't anything anybody could fix. It didn't matter, she decided, it would be worth getting poked and prodded, even getting a shot, to go to Miami.

"Did she say when we're going?"

"The appointment's in two weeks."

Chapter 22

AT SCHOOL THE NEXT MORNING they had a substitute. Miss Daniels was out with the flu.

After lunch, using the roll book, the substitute called on Elizabeth Martin to stand and continue reading, starting where they left off at lunchtime.

A whoop went up in the back of the room. Alex clamped his hand to his mouth, then did a silent cheer in his desk. His bottom wiggled, his top swayed, and his arms poked alternately in the air. He turned in his desk and grinned broadly at Buddy.

"Quiet, please," said the substitute. "Elizabeth."

Buddy stood, slowly, and steadied herself against her desktop. Her heart pounded in her chest and her head throbbed.

"Elizabeth, start at the top of page 79."

"Af, Af, After the . . . ba, battle, Presi . . . dent Lincoln saw . . ."

"That's was, Dumb Buddy," Alex said loudly. "A first grader knows was," he explained to Timmy.

"Oh my," cried the substitute. "You're Buddy? You're Buddy Marvin?" She ran her finger down the roll book. "It's Martin. I thought she said Marvin. Oh, I'm sorry, dear, you may sit down."

"Oh dear, you're the idiot," Alex cried, imitating the substitute's voice. "You may sit down, dear."

"Be quiet back there. Be quiet this instant."

The substitute, trying to move ahead, ran her finger down the roll and called out Alex's name. He grinned and stood up.

"Oh," she cried. "Never mind. Sit down, please."

Alex ignored her, picked up the history book, turned it upside down, and moved his finger heavily from word to word on the page. "Da," he said, letting his mouth hang open. "Da." He scratched his head. Timmy and Jeffery poked their books and scratched their heads.

"Sit down," the substitute cried.

The class giggled. A few let their lips loosen and their jaws go slack, uttered "duhs," poked at their textbooks, and scratched their heads.

"Stop it," screamed the substitute. She swooped toward Alex who dodged into his desk. She whirled on the class, her face red with fury. "You heartless little bastards," she screamed, then her eyes became round with horror, and she clamped her hand to her mouth.

The class broke into hoots and hollers. A few took up the imitation again. Alex made a spitball and shot it at Buddy. They all made them, targeting Buddy, each other, and the substitute as she swirled frantically around the room, screaming, "Sit down. Stop it. Sit down."

153

The teacher from the next classroom swung the door open with such force that the papers on Miss Daniels's desk were sucked up, then fluttered to the floor. He struck the first desktop he came to with a pointer. It snapped in half. There was the scramble of feet, then silence. "Every one of you will be punished for this." His voice was even and menacing. "Come with me." He took the substitute by the arm.

"I didn't know she was a girl," she whimpered up at him as he guided her out of the room.

A moment later, he reappeared. Whispers stopped, heads drooped, hands appeared and folded themselves on desktops.

Buddy sat in her desk, her hands gripping the far edge, her head down gasping for air. The deeper, more quickly she breathed, the more air she needed, as if she was trying to breathe through mud.

"Come with me," the teacher said, lifting her under both arms.

Buddy's legs would not hold her weight. He supported her as far as the outside hall, then he picked her up and carried her to the nurse's office.

The nurse spoke to her softly and made her cup her hands over her nose. When her breathing quieted, the nurse made her lie down on the cot. Then she wiped Buddy's face with a cool damp cloth until she fell asleep.

When school was over, the nurse woke her. "We tried to call your dad to come get you, but the operator said you don't have a phone. If you will wait till five, I'll take you home."

Buddy didn't want her father to know what had happened, she just wanted to see the Admiral. "No, ma'am, I'll take the bus home. I'm all right now."

"Are you sure, sweetheart?" The nurse stroked her hair.

"Yes, ma'am. I'm sure."

"Elizabeth," the nurse said, lifting her chin so their eyes met. "I heard what happened in there and I want you to know something."

"Yes 'am?"

"I'm sixty-three years old. I don't know you personally, but I've got four grown kids, eleven grandchildren, two great-grandchildren, and been nursing kids for forty years. You aren't dumb. I don't know what your problem is, but I know dumb when I see it. Dumb is in the eyes. Your eyes are bright with the light of a good mind."

Tears slid down Buddy's cheeks.

"I bet you're smarter than any kid in that class."

Buddy began to sob.

"That's it, baby," the nurse said gently. "You cry now, here with me, but the next time that little poop face pokes fun at you—punch him." The nurse's fist whizzed through the air.

Buddy laughed, then hiccupped. The nurse laughed, picked up a pillow and punched it, hard. "Hit him in the belly; hit him in the nose." She hugged Buddy. "Okay?"

"Yes ma'am," she said with a nod.

The nurse held the pillow up, and Buddy punched it as hard as she could then threw her arms around the nurse and the pillow. "Thank you."

~ ~ ~

155

Thunder rumbled as Buddy walked slowly to the bus stop. Children ran, screamed, and chased each other. No one noticed her. She stood in the narrow-arched shadow of a palm tree and watched them with curiosity. Like the way the spoonbills in the lagoon had looked at her and the Admiral. Children pushed and shoved to get on one of the buses. She saw Linda-Ellen Brown push the boy in front of her, then shriek and duck when he swung at her. Linda-Ellen had been Buddy's friend in the third grade. When Buddy failed that year, Linda-Ellen never spoke to her again. That seemed so long ago that Buddy couldn't remember what having a friend her own age had felt like.

Suddenly, her books shot out from between her arm and her hip and splayed out on the grass.

"You got us all in trouble, Dumb Buddy," Alex scolded. "We gotta write essays and stay fifteen minutes after school every day for a week cleaning up the room. It's all your fault, 'cause you're so stupid."

Buddy's hands squeezed into fists.

"You gonna hit me?" Alex hooted and danced in front of her, shadowboxing.

She relaxed her hands and squatted down to pick up her books. Alex kicked them away.

She stood up and started walking. Alex skipped around her and danced alongside as she left the school yard, walked Copeland Avenue to the Broadway Circle, and crossed it to the highway.

At the traffic circle he stopped, but called out, "Dumb

Buddy is teacher's pet," until she was too far away to hear him.

Thunder rumbled nearer, and it was raining by the time she got to the bridge to home.

Lightning flashed.

"One one-thousand, two one-thousand, three one-thousand . . ."

Boom.

She flinched. "Three miles," she said, walking faster.

Boom.

Buddy ducked and covered her ears, then started to run, stopped, took her sandals off, stepped onto the highway, and ran toward home.

Lightning flashed so near that the trees, for an instant, had no color. The world went white, then sounded as if it had blown up.

Buddy shrieked, threw her arms over her head, dropped to the ground and rolled into a tight ball.

Brakes squealed. The school bus driver flung the doors open, jumped down, and raced across the highway. "Are you hurt?" she asked, touching Buddy's shoulder.

"No, ma'am. I'm afraid of storms."

"Isn't everybody?" The driver asked, helping her up.

The driver went to her bus stop first. When Buddy stepped off, the sun was out and steam rose from the pavement. She ran down the hill, up the ramp, across the kitchen and living room to the Admiral's door. She rapped softly and stuck her head in. He wasn't there.

"Admiral?" she called at the bathroom door, pushed it

open slowly, then dashed back through the kitchen and down the ramp.

Her father was on his stomach on the deck of his boat leaning over the engine, the insides of which he had exposed.

"Hi," she said.

He looked up. "Why are you wet?"

"I waited for the bus in the rain." She looked down at her feet.

"How was school?"

"We had a substitute."

"Uh-huh." His head was back in the engine.

"Where's the Admiral?"

Kirk pointed the wrench he was holding. "I put him on the porch."

Her grandfather's head was against the pillow her father had jammed down between his shoulders and the back of the chair. His mouth was open and he was snoring.

"Admiral?" she whispered.

There was a momentary pause in his ragged breathing, then it started again.

"Admiral, it's me." She touched his shoulder.

His head snapped up. He blinked and squinted at her.

"Hi," she said, pushing herself up to sit on the porch railing.

"How are you?" he asked, running his hand over his crusty eyes, then rubbing them vigorously.

"Okay. You were asleep."

"Do I get a hug anyway?"

She hopped down, knelt beside his chair, wrapped her arms around his waist, and put her face against his unbandaged shoulder.

"How was school?"

"Awful."

"Alex again?"

Her head nodded against his shoulder.

"I'm sorry, honey." He rubbed a circle on her back and kissed the top of her head. "You're wet."

"I walked most of the way home.

"Ah ha." He put his cheek against her hair.

Buddy nudged in closer, waiting, but he said no more.

His skin smelled moldy and stale, like damp clothes in the hamper too long. His hair was matted and oily, and he hadn't shaved for a week or more. His shirt smelled like the decaying odor of river mud when the tide was out; a smell she used to like.

At the sound of her father's step on the porch stairs, Buddy jumped to her feet and, without thinking, hopped behind the Admiral's chair, putting him between herself and her father. As soon as she did, she was sorry.

Kirk stared at them for a moment, then his expression changed, hardened. "Dinner's going to be early tonight," he said. "I've got to be up at five, so I want to get it over with and get to bed." He went into the house, letting the door bang shut behind him.

Chapter 23

BUDDY PULLED HER BLUE, Swiss-dot church dress off a hanger in the back of the closet. She held it out, snapped it in the air, fanned away the dust and sneezed. Its white lace-trimmed bib and the cuffs on the short sleeves were yellowing. She held it up even with her shoulders. The hem was still out of the back where she had caught it getting down from the truck. But even where it hung down, it did not touch her knees. She put it back on the hanger and closed the closet door.

Osceola was tucked into himself at the glass watching her.

"You hungry?" She lowered her hand through the water slowly and poked through the sand with a finger until she found a clam. She put her face near the crab and grinned at him through the glass, "I'm getting ready to go to Miami."

~ ~ ~

The Admiral was in his chair in the shade on the front porch, snoring softly. She tiptoed over and kissed his cheek.

He opened his eyes, grunted, and rubbed the back of his neck. "You cooking for that crab of yours?"

"Yeah. He's getting little claws." She smashed the clam with the hammer, picked the shell fragments out of the meat, and began to dice it. She looked up at him. "Admiral, did you know that when their claws grow back, they is under a clear little cap-thing?"

"I've seen it a time or two."

"Neat, ain't it?"

"Yep. When he molts, that shield will drop off and he'll have himself a nice new set of claws."

"I'll let him go then. Soon as he can feed himself, or after my science report, if he molts first. I hope he don't, I want the kids to see his claws under them caps." She scooped the pieces of clam into her palm. "After I feed him, you want to play some cards or something?"

"I don't think so. Looking at cards makes my eyes hurt."

"Want to go for a walk? Smallwood's is closed. We could go sit under the store and watch for dolphins or something."

"Maybe later, okay?"

"Yes, sir." She nodded and watched his face for a sign that he really meant later this time, or at least for the twinkle in his eye that would mean he felt better, that he had made the turn and was headed back to be with her.

He yawned.

She stood up, folded her fingers over on the clam and put her arms around his neck, her cheek against his cheek. "I gotta go see Iris or Miss Nancy 'bout borrowing something to wear to Miami. I'll be back by lunch, okay?"

"I ain't seen you in a dress in years." He rubbed the bumps of her spine. "You sure was beautiful in a dress."

"Ah, Admiral, a dress ain't gonna make me beautiful. I ain't even sure it'll make me look like a girl."

He took her arms. "You're the prettiest girl in Collier County and getting prettier every day. You just wait, won't be long before I gotta sit out here with a shotgun across my knees to keep the boys away. Bang, bang." He fired his fingers at two trees.

Buddy blushed. "If boys is all like Alex and his friends, I ain't ever gonna want one. We can both sit out here and shoot at 'em." She scrunched into the chair with him and leaned her head against his shoulder. "If I ever do get married, will you come and live with me?"

"It will be mighty hard to find you a husband if he's gonna get me in the bargain."

"Then I ain't getting married," she said, holding her hand out so the juice from the clam trickled through her fingers and dripped on the porch. "Ever."

Short, round, Iris Smallwood couldn't find a dress to fit Buddy, so she made her pick a skirt from her closet. Buddy chose a faded, pleated, plaid one because it looked like her fishing cap, though she didn't plan to wear them together.

Iris took it in at the waist, let the hem out, and pressed it. When it was finished, they walked over to the Blue Heron Motel where Iris's aunt, Nancy Smallwood Hanson, added a white blouse with a long scarf attached to the edges of a stand-up collar. They tied and retied it until they got a bow that drooped evenly on both sides. When they finished, Buddy looked like a twelve-year-old, bare-footed schoolmarm. She looked from one to the other, her long bangs snagging her eyelashes.

"Well," Nancy and Iris said together and glanced at each other. "That will be fine for Miami," Nancy said. Iris nodded.

"Do you have some white sandals?" Iris asked.

"Yes, ma'am. My school sandals is mostly white."

"Good. Then all we need is a barrette for your bangs," Iris said, pulling them to one side and turning Buddy's head this way and that by her chin. "A red one. I have one down at the store."

Early the next morning, Buddy heard Jane shift gears when she came off the stop sign at Mamie Street. She grabbed her sandals from the closet, the barrette off her dresser, shouted "bye, crab," dashed out of her room, and burst into the Admiral's. "She's here."

A sandal dangled from each pinky as she snapped the barrette into her hair. She grinned at her grandfather then did a little jig on her toes, her arms poking the air, sandals bouncing. "Just think, Admiral, all the way to Miami."

He smiled and held his arms out. "I found something I want you to have." He opened the drawer in the little table beside his bed and took out a small box. He handed it to her but held her hands to keep her from opening it. "When I was in school, the first of my growed teeth I lost was an eyetooth." He lowered his voice and winked. "Got it knocked out fighting. Back then I figured an eyetooth was worth saving, so I picked it out of the dirt and kept it." He let her hands go. "It's brought me good luck ever since. You take it now."

Buddy opened the little box, lifted the tissue, and took out the tooth. She closed it in her fist and looked at him. "I wish you could keep an eye on me through this tooth."

"Maybe I can. Ain't ever tried."

There were two short beeps from the road.

She stood up. "Admiral, try. Okay?"

The pocket in the skirt had a small hole in the bottom. Buddy dashed to her room, dumped her bottom drawer out on her bed and sorted through it until she found the white patent leather purse that had gone with the church dress. She opened it, dropped the tooth in, snapped it closed and ran out. At the Admiral's door, she held up the purse. "It's in here. I love you." She waved the purse and was gone.

Buddy held her purse in her lap and focused on the arrow-straight, brown water canal until it seemed to be the thing moving instead of them. She remembered there was a mangrove branch slung so low it had hooked a blue crab trap buoy. She watched for it.

When they reached the blinking light at the intersection of 29 and 41, she knew they would turn right, east into the sun. She knew Stevens's was five miles and that they would pass a sign: Miami 72. Buddy knew where she was.

Two cars, one with a New Jersey tag and one from Iowa, were already in Stevens's lot.

"Tourists," Jane hissed. "Their money keeps that old fart in business."

Buddy clamped her hand over her mouth to stifle a laugh, thought of Annie and Lucie jumping through hoops, and dropped her hand.

"I filed a report with the Marine Patrol. Hopefully, they'll jerk his license and take them away from him."

"Will they let them go?"

"No, they'll move them somewhere else where they will be properly taken care of."

"Why can't they just let them go?"

"It is assumed that once an animal has been tamed, it loses its ability to care for itself in the wild. That makes us responsible for what we tame, forever."

Buddy looked back at Stevens's. "Do you think that's true? That they can't take care of themselves anymore?"

"It is for most animals, especially ones taken young, but I'm not so sure about animals as smart as dolphins that were captured as adults. It's pretty hard to believe they've forgotten how to feed themselves."

"My crab eats out of my hand."

"That's all right. Once he's back in the ocean, he'll go right back to finding his own food. He's not tame, he's trusting and that's easy to get over."

165

~ ~ ~

Sawgrass stretched away to their right, ending against a distant wall of mangroves. Buddy leaned back and watched the scenery sweep by. Near the highway, in open shallow pools, egrets and herons clustered, poised, eyes locked on the water, motionless as statues until, with a lightning-fast thrust of a head, one then another would catch a fish, like Seminoles spearfishing.

"Are you excited about seeing Miami?" Jane asked after a long silence.

Buddy's head bobbed and her barrette fell out. She swept her bangs to one side and snapped the barrette closed on them.

Jane glanced at her watch. "We're a little late so we have to go straight to Dr. Wheeler's, but we'll see the city right after that, okay?"

They rode a while longer in silence before Buddy turned to Jane. "Do you really think this doctor can fix me? Nobody could fix the Admiral."

"What does that have to do with you?"

"Dad said you said I had a learning disability. The Admiral's spine getting crushed was called a disability by the insurance company."

"I said I *think* you have a learning disability. But it's not the same thing. His is a physical disability. And if you do have an LD, as they call it, Dr. Wheeler can help you."

Ellen Wheeler cleared two chairs, one of books and the other of more books, a stuffed raccoon, and a musical

166

bear. She put them all on top of her cluttered desk behind a sign that read: Dyslexics of the World Untie.

She was a large, tidy woman with a bubble of soft blonde hair and cheeks that inflated like shiny pink balloons when she smiled, which was nearly all the time. She leaned forward so her head appeared above the books as if it rested on them, and smiled at Buddy. "Miss Conroy tells me she thinks we have a problem in common, you and me."

Buddy looked at Jane, then back at Dr. Wheeler. "We do?"

"Yes." Dr. Wheeler picked up the raccoon and touched the end of its nose. "She thinks you're dyslexic like me."

"What is that?"

Dr. Wheeler smiled. "Just a different way of seeing things." She put the raccoon against the stack of books next to the bear, who let out two slow notes like a sigh. "When I was your age, they thought I was retarded. I was teased by other children and left out of games."

Buddy ducked her head and scraped her toes back and forth inside her sandals.

Dr. Wheeler came around her desk, knelt in front of Buddy and lifted her chin. "They were wrong about me and they are wrong about you. We are very smart, we are. I've got some tests here. If you are dyslexic, they will show it. And if you are, I'll show you how to get around it. Okay?"

Buddy nodded.

Dr. Wheeler squeezed Buddy's hand. "I promise, you

167

will be able to read and write and do arithmetic." She stood up, her cheeks pink and glowing. "How many grades have you failed?"

"One. So far." Buddy scraped her sandals off, put her hands under her thighs and dug her toes into the carpet.

"I failed two," Dr. Wheeler said.

"You did?"

"Yes, ma'am. Now I have a Ph.D. Do you know what that is?"

"Yes 'am. Jane here's getting one on crabs."

The two women burst out laughing. Buddy smiled and waited until they were quiet. "I ain't too good at tests."

"Oh, these aren't like the tests you take in school. Some are even fun."

"You two go to work," Jane said, getting up. "I have errands to do." She walked to the door, turned and gave Buddy a thumbs-up. "See you in a couple of hours."

"Now, the first test is a game that lets me interpret what you see." Dr. Wheeler sorted through a drawer and came up with a plastic bag full of small square tiles with designs on them. She shook them out in the space she'd cleared on her desk then looked at Buddy. "Do you know that Albert Einstein, the smartest man who ever lived, was dyslexic?" She selected tiles and placed them in a line, end to end. "So was Rodin, a brilliant artist, and Woodrow Wilson, one of our presidents and . . ."

Buddy interrupted. "Was Teddy Roosevelt?"

"I don't think so." She smiled. "But he was smart enough to have been."

~ ~ ~

"Well?" Jane poked her head into the office. Buddy and Dr. Wheeler were laughing. "How did it go?"

Buddy held her hand up, to silence Ellen Wheeler, and grinned. "I've got it. I'm dyslexic."

Jane laughed and hugged her. "I guess that's wonderful."

"And watch this. I can subtract." Buddy placed a recipe card over the tens and the hundreds columns of the problem 279 from 543. "Nine from three will not go," Buddy whispered to herself. "Strike, change, make a teen. Nine from thirteen is four." She wrote four and moved the card left a column. "Seven from three will not go, strike, change, make a teen. Seven from thirteen is six," she said, but wrote nine.

"Watch your sixes and nines," Dr. Wheeler said.

"Oops." Buddy erased the nine and carefully made a six. "Nine from thirteen is four, seven from thirteen is six, and two from four is two. Two hundred and sixty-four." She slapped the pencil down and threw her arms up. "How 'bout that?"

Jane and Dr. Wheeler applauded.

"The secret is keeping the other columns covered so that the numbers can't be reversed. And remember," Dr. Wheeler said to Buddy, "be extra careful when you see a six or a nine and a five or a two. We tend to turn those numbers upside down."

Dr. Wheeler had given Buddy a folder of instructions to parents and instructions to teachers, a workbook called

Solving Language Difficulties, and the seventy-five dollars in Monopoly money she'd won doing subtraction problems. "Take your pick," she indicated the priced toys in plastic bags thumbtacked to a corkboard on the wall behind the office door.

Buddy handed the money back. "No, thank you, ma'am, I got this book." She ran her hand over the bright orange cover. "I won't have time to play with toys."

Outside, Buddy stopped with her hand on the car door. "Thank you for bringing me here."

"My pleasure, madam," Jane said, and made a sweeping bow before ducking into the driver's seat and leaning across to unlock Buddy's door. "Come on, I've got a surprise for you."

"You do? What?"

"Ah, ah." Jane wagged a finger. "Patience."

Chapter 24

"A WHALE?" Buddy smacked her hands together and whirled in her seat to face Jane. "A real whale?"

Jane nodded. "This is the Seaquarium and they've had this whale since May. His name is Hugo. He's an orca, a killer whale. A small whale, as whales go."

"He's a killer?"

"Most whales eat plankton; killer whales hunt in large groups called pods and eat fish and seals," she said, paying for their tickets.

As they came through the gate, an announcement came over the loudspeaker: "Ladies and Gentlemen, the dolphin show will begin in the Seaquarium's center tank in ten minutes."

"Come on," Jane said, "I wanted you to see a real dolphin show."

When they entered the cool, dark entrance to the center tank, Buddy stopped. "Was that a real dolphin?" she asked, pointing at the white dolphin mounted high on the wall over a machine that made plastic replicas of dolphins and whales.

"Yes," Jane said without looking up. "That's Carolina Snowball. She was captured off the coast of South Carolina."

"Did they kill her and put her up there?"

"They didn't kill her on purpose. She got sick and died, then they put her up there. People came to the Seaquarium just to see the world's only white dolphin. They still want to see her."

"I'm surprised Mr. Blossom didn't do that to poor Osceola," Buddy said, as they climbed the circular concrete staircase to the top of the main tank.

"I'm sure it's only because he didn't think of it," Jane said.

Buddy hooked her arms over the railing and peered down into the deep, clear water. Dolphins swept by as if caught in an eddy of their own making. She turned to look at Jane. "Do you think it's right, that they caught that white dolphin and brought her here?"

"No. I don't."

Buddy straightened and turned to face Jane. "I don't remember my mother, but I think she was like you. Inside," Buddy tapped her chest with a finger, "in here, she was like you. She don't come into my head so much since I met you. I think she must be resting better knowing you're my friend."

Tears filled Jane's eyes. "She must have been very special to have had a daughter like you." She turned Buddy back facing the tank, wrapped her arms around her shoulders, and put her chin on top of Buddy's head.

A young woman in a bathing suit climbed a ladder to a platform above the tank, welcomed them to the Top Deck Dolphin Show, then blew a whistle and raised her arms. Seven dolphins sailed into the air, turned somersaults, and disappeared again.

Buddy suddenly felt as if she was going to cry. As if a somersault, a joyous act, had become just a circle back to where you started. She turned to look up at Jane. "Dad said animals is missing the parts of their brains that let them miss their homes and families. He said scientists found that out. Is that true?"

"Some scientists believe that. I think animals are just missing the ability to tell us what they miss and how they feel, and we conveniently ignore what they try to show us."

Buddy turned back in time to see Flipper, the star of the show, jump twenty-three feet in the air for a fish. "Do you think that after a while they finally give up thinking about it?" she asked, clapping politely with the rest of the audience.

"Probably, they do," Jane said. But when Buddy glanced at her, she saw the same look of kindness and pity she'd seen when she had asked if Annie and Lucie could get dolphin pox.

In the next show, Salty, the sea lion, played with his trainer by catching the beach ball on the tip of his nose, balancing it, then launching it back with a flick of his head.

"It would be more fair, and a lot more interesting, if the trainer had to catch it and balance it on the end of his nose, too, don't you think?" Jane whispered.

Buddy giggled and nodded.

The trainer rolled out a sheet of red plastic, wet it with a couple of pails of water, then signaled Salty who shot up onto one side of the long raft, slid the entire length, and dropped into the tank at the other end.

"Does the trainer have to go next?" Buddy asked and grinned at Jane.

Hugo, the killer whale, had been at the Seaquarium for six months. He was being trained but, as yet, there was no show. It seemed to Buddy that the faces of the people who came in were full, first of curiosity, then awe, then pity as they stood and watched him slowly move around and around his tank.

And as much as Buddy had wanted to see him, she found she couldn't bear the sight of him there alone in a pool that was only a few feet deeper than he was long. She told Jane she was ready to go home.

It was nearly dark when they passed Stevens's, but Buddy straightened a little as if it were possible to catch a glimpse of Annie. "How long will it be before the Marine Patrol people take them away?" she asked, still looking back at the dark pond.

"January, at the earliest. It will take that long to finish the bureaucratic b.s. necessary to revoke his license and find another place willing to take them. And if Lucie's really pregnant, they may want to wait until after the baby comes."

"I wonder if Annie and Lucie can call the sea up in their heads like I can call up Momma and the Admiral? If they can, do you think the memory makes it easier or worse?"

"Worse, I would think."

"Me, too. And Hugo. He must hate being in that little pool instead of the ocean."

"Yes, I'm sure he does. It is wrong of us to take away his freedom. But maybe, if we try, we can learn how wrong it is from Hugo."

Buddy thought about that for awhile. "Jane," she said, after a few minutes, "do you get paid for finding out if stone crabs is being used up?"

She nodded. "I work for the state of Florida, but they pay me with money they get from the federal government, tax money."

Buddy put her head back against the seat. "Did the Seaquarium have to pay anybody for Hugo or Flipper or Snowball?"

"No, they caught them or paid someone to catch them."

"You know what? I think the government ought to make places like the Seaquarium give some of all that money they make to people like you. It ain't fair they can take them from the ocean and not have to pay to find out if they're using 'em all up."

"Did anyone ever tell you you're brilliant?"

"Nope." Buddy grinned. "That's one thing nobody ever told me."

~ ~ ~

Kirk was sitting on the porch with his feet on the railing, drinking a beer. He dropped them and stood up when they parked. "How'd it go?" he called.

Buddy jumped out of the car and ran toward him. "Great," she said, passing him on the steps. She jerked open the screen door and ran to her grandfather's room.

The Admiral was asleep. Buddy stood beside his bed and whispered his name. He snored on. She watched his chest move up and down for awhile, then crossed to his door, and turned. "We're dyslexic, Admiral," she said softly, then smiled. "You and me and Einstein."

Buddy crossed the living room but stopped at the kitchen door when she heard Jane say, ". . . it's not a form of retardation. Einstein was dyslexic."

"Where does it come from?" she heard her father ask.

"It's inherited."

"I don't see things backward and neither did my wife, Elizabeth."

"Your father does," Jane said.

Buddy coughed, pushed the door open and went in. Her father and Jane were sitting across from each other at the table drinking beer. She grinned at them.

Kirk turned and smiled at her, but it faded quickly. He reached and took her hand. "All these years . . .," he said, then after a long pause, ". . . you and Dad." Then for the first time in all of Buddy's memory, her father hugged her.

Chapter 25

THE STONE CRAB SEASON, so far, had not been good and Buddy's father was short-tempered because of it. She kept out of his way when she could.

Then that Saturday, from the kitchen window, she'd seen her father's boat coming back into the docks before noon. *It must have really been a bad day,* she thought, retreating to her room where she stayed to work on her science report until she heard him in the shed, sawing wood.

Buddy felt safe in moving to the front porch to start work on the poster she needed of the stone crab's life cycle. She'd been at it for a while when she heard her father hammering something at the back of the house. She crept down the east side, pressed her stomach to the wall behind the croton hedge, and peeked around the corner. He had nails pinched between his lips. A stack of short boards leaned against the wall under her bedroom window. He selected one, fitted it across the one he had just nailed, and pounded it into place.

She pulled her head in and moved quietly back to the front porch. When she opened the screen door to go into the house to ask the Admiral why her father was nailing up her window, she knocked over the jar of water she'd been using to clean her paintbrush.

She passed the bathroom on her way to the kitchen for paper towels and heard water running in the bathroom sink. She knew her grandfather was bathing himself as best he could because he hated asking his son to do it.

"Damn it, Buddy," her father shouted, "come out here."

She dashed to the kitchen, grabbed a streamer of paper towels, circled back, and burst out onto the porch.

He was standing on the step with his hands on his hips staring down at the papers, paints, the overturned jar, and the blue stain on the wood.

"I'm going to clean it up," she said, dropping to her knees to wipe the wet spot. The cracks in the wood snagged strips of toweling. She tried to dig those out with the end of her paintbrush, but it was too thick.

"You're only making it worse. I needed you to help me. Now you have this to do," he snapped and walked away in a flurry of blown leaves.

Buddy stood up and actually raised her hand as if she could catch his shirt and stop him. Ask him to wait. Tell him it would only take a minute. But she dropped her hand, rubbed the white cords of skin on her knees where they had been pressed into the cracks, and realized that she didn't want to help him, or be with him.

Buddy, her arms loaded with paints, brushes, the

178

empty jar, her notebook, and the unfinished poster, stopped at her door and stared at the dark X the two boards made against her sunlit window. She felt as if it already marked the work she'd done a failure, and her, too. She put all she carried down on the foot of her bed, crawled onto the bedspread, and rolled herself into a ball. She wound her T-shirt into a knot and held it hard against her stomach. The curtains on her window flared out suddenly, then were sucked back flat against the screen. The crab appeared at the entrance to his tube, raised himself up, then scuttled to the side of the tank and looked out at her.

The hammering continued, hurting her head. She reached up and felt along the headboard to the bedpost for her red plaid cap. She got up, put it on, and slipped out of the house.

Only two boats were at the docks, her father's and one other. She paddled the pitpan out the channel and around the point before starting the motor. Outside the harbor, a gusty breeze chopped the creamy, pistachio green water. It lapped at the low sides of the pitpan, splashing in and down her bare legs to swirl and roll around her feet. She slapped one foot rhythmically in the puddle as if she were keeping time to music.

On the back side of the island, the waters calmed, but the warm breeze pressed her shirt to her back and puffed it out in front like wind in a sail. The clouds were long and round like rolling surf and they passed quickly overhead in a wide arc.

179

It was ten twisty miles to Stevens's. In the open, wide stretches of the river, she could push the pitpan up to twelve or fourteen miles an hour, but through the narrow mangrove tunnels, she puttered slowly, looking for birds, but this day, though they should be busy building nests, there were none. The silence was creepy.

At Stevens's Buddy crept up the side of the levee and looked both ways. She was about to dart across when an airboat's engine exploded to life twenty yards to her right. Buddy jerked her head in like a turtle.

There were no customers on the benches of the airboat as it headed downriver past her hiding place. She hunkered low in the willow stand and watched until it disappeared into the sawgrass. She was just ready to try to cross to the cover of the sea grape when the other two airboats' engines whined to a start and whizzed downriver in the wake of the first. Stevens's son puttered after them in a little dory, the sound of its motor lost in the roar of airboat engines.

When there were no people and no more boats, Buddy dashed across the levee to the culvert. She slid into the water and patted the surface with her palm. "Annie," she whispered.

A dolphin's blowhole appeared, opened, and blasted misty, warm air over her. Annie rolled on her side to show her grin, then rolled back and slid her dorsal fin into Buddy's hand.

Buddy put a finger to her lips in warning, then wrapped her hands around the fin. Annie whisked her to the shallow end of the pond, and deposited her waist-deep and giggling, soundlessly, in the muddy water. Annie ran aground beside her.

The sun winked through the clouds one last time and disappeared.

From the far end of the pond, Lucie surfaced and eased toward them until she was near enough to touch. When Buddy put her hand out, Lucie nudged it with her snout then backed away, but slowly enough for Buddy to see the small, dry, white lump at the side of her mouth. She felt as if her heart had stopped.

Annie's head was in the water bumping against her hip. "Oh, please," she whispered, running her hands over the dolphin's slick, cool, gray skin, "don't let it happen to Annie. Not Annie."

Buddy found nothing. Relief, warm, as if the sun had broken out again, spread over her. Her Annie was all right.

Annie seemed to think so, too. She lifted her head up, then dropped it with enough force to roll Buddy over with the wave.

Buddy righted herself and splashed her back. "You want to play, huh?" She splashed her again then bellied into deeper water like a gator.

Annie wiggled herself backward out of the muddy, shallow water and came up beside Buddy, slipping her fin into Buddy's cupped hand.

The first pumps of Annie's tail sucked Buddy's legs down, then lifted them again, suspending her above the dolphin's back. Annie took her gently along the show pool side of the pond, then faster and faster, so when they made the sweeping turn at the parking lot end of the pond and started down the levee side, she was nearly full speed, her tail pumping furiously. Buddy held her head back to keep the water out of her mouth. Her chin threw off a rooster tail of water like a slalom skier. When they started around the second time, Lucie joined them, on the inside, making a tighter circle.

When the rush of water against her chest broke Buddy's hold, Annie stopped. Their backwash rolled over Buddy, dunking her. She sputtered to the surface across Annie's snout and was carried toward the shallows at the cattail end of the pond. When her feet touched bottom, Annie sank out from under her. A moment later, she shot into the air from the center of the pond and did a somersault. When she came up again, she lifted up on her tail and spun like a water spout. Buddy stood on her tiptoes, knee-deep and dripping, threw her arms out wide and spun like the dolphin. When Annie flopped back in the water, Buddy did, too.

From the river, she heard the dory's little motor and the sound of men laughing. Annie and Lucy sank beneath the surface. Buddy stood and stepped deeper into the cattails. From there she could see the three airboat drivers and Stevens's son leave the dory tied to the dock and march, single file, up the ramp and across the lot toward the gift shop. She held her breath until they disappeared and wondered what they had done with the airboats.

The wind had been coming, off and on, in gusts, calm one minute, agitated the next. Now, for the first time, a light sprinkle of rain began to pock the surface of the pond. Buddy sat in the water with Annie nosed in beside her, put her head back and caught raindrops on her tongue. When it began to rain harder, she put her forehead against the dolphin's. "I had a wonderful time, Annie, but it looks like it's gonna storm." She kissed her cheek. "I guess I'd better start for home."

Annie followed her as she swam back. At the culvert, Buddy turned and stroked Annie's face. "My friend Jane is trying to get you out of here 'cause this is such an awful place to live." It hurt to even think about that. Buddy closed her eyes for a second. "I wish you could just go with me. I wish you lived in the bay where the water feels good and the fish ain't dead, and you could come to Smallwood's to swim with me."

Annie's smile was too much for her. She hoisted herself up onto the drain pipe. "I'll go now, I guess." She stepped up on the levee and turned. Her pale hair, rusty with silt, produced rivulets of water, which ran down her face and neck. Everywhere, crooked little streams made their way down her body, down her arms and legs, dripping finally off her fingers and feet and chin. The warm wind gusted suddenly and chilled her.

The dolphin rolled on her side and moved her flipper up and down.

"Bye, Annie," she whispered, raising her hand like a person making a pledge. She held it there for a moment, then folded her fingers and let her arm drop. She turned and crossed the few feet of dirt and crushed shells that separated the pond from the river to the sea.

183

Chapter 26

THE RAIN FROM THE FIRST BRIEF SQUALL had stopped, but the wind gusts, when they came across the open prairie, were strong enough to blow the pitpan sideways across the water. One blew her stern first into the sawgrass, where she stalled. Buddy raised the motor and pulled strands of weeds off the prop. In the quiet, she could hear thunder rumble. She shook her finger at the swirling sky. "Just wait 'til I'm home."

When she came off the trail into the river, she saw all three of Stevens's airboats strung on a line and lashed at each end to the mangroves with ropes. She remembered the men laughing and decided maybe this was a joke they were playing on Mr. Blossom, though she didn't believe anybody would have the nerve.

When the second line of squalls hit, it brought pouring rain and stronger winds. Buddy was near one of the dead-end channels. She swung the bow toward the entrance, cut her engine, and guided the pitpan into the narrow opening. Once inside, she pulled her cap low, humped her shoulders, wrapped her arms around her drawn-up knees and put her chin in the crack between them. The low, steady whine of the wind whirling above her and the creaking of swaying limbs were the only sounds she heard until the sound of a boat's motor was carried back to her on the wind from downriver.

Her head jerked up. "Hello," she cried. "I'm here." She pulled the pitpan, hand over hand, backward out of the channel. When the stern poked out into the river, the wind caught her cap and blew it upstream. It hit the water, whirled in an eddy until it was so waterlogged, the wind gave it up to the current, which floated it back toward her. There was no sign of a boat. She waited for her cap to drift into reach, wrung it out, and put it on, then started her engine and pushed back out into the river.

She tried to keep going. Where the river was narrow and shielded by mangroves, it wasn't too bad, but where it fanned out, the wind got too strong for the pitpan's little motor, and she was blown into the trees or jammed against sandbars. The howl of the wind frightened her; the rain stung her arms and legs and she was cold.

It was nearly dark when she saw a small opening in the mangroves. She jumped overboard and pulled the pitpan, stern first, into the tight black, dead-end tunnel, then she crawled back in and curled into a knot on the bottom of the boat. The low-slung branches creaked above her head and small spiders, knocked loose from the leaves and branches of the mangrove trees, went to work webbing her to the deck. It was wet and warm in the tunnel, and the wind didn't touch her. After a while, she grew used to the howl and the frantic frenzy of the branches high above her head. She watched them in the waning light.

When the sound of the wind became a roar like that of a semi sweeping past on the highway, she covered her ears, closed her eyes, and wished she'd brought the Admiral's eyetooth. She tried to see his face on the black back of her lids, but he wasn't there and the roar grew louder, nearer. "Admiral," she cried. "Momma. Anybody," she sobbed.

She pulled her cap down as low as she could and squeezed the knot she'd made of herself tighter. Her ears popped. "I'm scared, Admiral," she said.

"Don't be afraid," she told herself in a deeper voice.

A moment later, the hair on her arms and legs stood straight up, pulled at by the wind, and in the next instant, it felt as if someone had covered her nose and mouth with cold, dead lips and sucked the air from her lungs. The branches above her head cracked, splintered off, and crashed somewhere else, exposing the sky. Eyes wide, she gasped for air and screamed in terror as the black funnel cloud swept upriver.

Then over the receding roar, Buddy thought she heard a shout. Someone shouting. Shouting her name.

"I'm here," she cried, scrambled forward to the bow of the pitpan and leaned out.

Twenty yards downstream, a pale arc of light from a dropped flashlight was shining up from the bottom of a boat, she could see the tops of white rubber boots and a man's knees. She took her cap off and waved it back and forth just under the branches, low over the water. "I'm here," she called. "I'm here, please." But the wind carried her voice upstream.

The boat drew nearer, until, when it was only yards away, she recognized it as the dory from Stevens's and the driver as her father. He was doubled over, rocking back and forth with his arms locked over his head.

"Daddy. Daddy," she cried, crawled off the bow and dropped into the water.

Kirk's head jerked up when Buddy grabbed onto the side of the dory. In the glow from the flashlight, she could see that his eyes were red and swollen. Blood from a gash on his forehead washed down his left cheek and neck, staining his denim shirt. "Daddy, I'm sorry," she said, "I didn't know a storm was coming."

"Thank God," he cried, grabbing her hand. "The tornado. Oh, thank God. I thought I'd lost you."

He leaned toward her but before he could lift her into the dory, which was still moving slowly upstream, it passed over a tangle of branches snagging her legs as if the river itself was trying to claim her, tear her back from her father.

"Daddy," she cried out as the boat moved on.

He only had her fingers and his grip was painfully tight, pulling her arm till it strained to leave its socket. She tried to kick her feet free but instead ripped her wet fingers from her father's fist and went under.

It was silent and black as death beneath the surface.

Overcome with panic, she flailed blindly until her hands struck mud. She gasped in surprise, swallowing water and choking before she realized she was facing down and twisted in the other direction to force her hand out into the wind. Her father had jumped overboard. A second after her hand broke the surface, he caught her under each of her arms and lifted her and the tangle of tree branches into the air. He pulled her close and crushed her to his chest. "I'm so sorry, Buddy. So sorry," he whispered against her ear. Warm tears struck her shoulder.

After her father snapped away the branches that clung to her feet, he waded, carrying her, to the dory, which had been blown aground on a sandbar. Kirk pulled it off and physically pointed it toward home. At the tunnel where Buddy had wedged the pitpan, her father went over the side again to lash it with a rope to the mangroves.

The river offered some protection from the high winds, giving a false sense of the storm. Where the river met the bay, huge waves rolled in, foam and spray filled the air so much they could not see Chokoloskee. Her father made a sweeping turn back into calmer water.

Buddy, shouting to make herself heard, pointed to the shellmound that rose up behind the old cistern near the first bend in the river. Together they carried the dory up through the white mangroves to the top, turned it on its side against a tree, and crawled beneath it.

Her father wrapped his arms around her again, pressing her head to his chest. "Try to sleep," he said, against her ear.

~ ~ ~

It was more the silence than the light of dawn that woke her. She found herself tucked into the S curve of her father's body, as if she'd been sitting in his lap and they had fallen over. His right arm was across her shoulders, his other arm was her pillow.

She carefully lifted his arm and crawled out from under the dory, stood and stretched.

The gronk-call of the Great Blue heron she scared woke him. "How's it look out there?" he asked, rubbing the print of her head on his arm.

"Bay's still a little choppy." She squatted down in front of him.

"Are you okay?" he asked, taking her hands.

She nodded.

"I thought I'd lost you last night," he said softly, keeping his head down. "When I found your boat gone and knew I'd let you go off without knowing about the storm, I . . . I was terrified." He pulled her into his arms and kissed the top of her head. "Stevens's said he hadn't seen you, but I knew, after the way I acted, that's where you'd go. That's where I would have gone. I borrowed the dory thinking I could catch up."

"You almost did," she said. "I was in the tunnel sitting out a squall when you passed the first time."

A pained look crossed his face. "Please forgive me," he said, and it sounded as if he meant he was sorry for not finding her then. But she knew that wasn't what he meant at all. She remembered what the Admiral had said in the ambulance about him loving them, just not how to do it right. Now she understood. And she realized her father thought he'd cared for her all wrong. He was asking her to forgive him for having let her love for him slip away. He didn't know it hadn't. He didn't know she'd been waiting.

"There's nothing to forgive," she said, and for her that was true.

Chapter 27

KIRK SCRAWLED A NOTE on a piece of Buddy's notebook paper and sent it with her when she went the final time to Jane's to finish her report.

Jane burst out laughing. "I'm sorry," she said. "It's an invitation to have Thanksgiving dinner with you. That's very nice. I'm not laughing at that. But it says at the bottom, 'If you have a special recipe for turkey, it would make a nice change.' "

"It sure would," Buddy laughed. "We ain't never had any turkey we could chew."

"Well, I still have all my own teeth; I'll be brave and accept the invitation. However, I don't know anything about cooking turkeys. But tell him thanks and, though I bet he already suspects this, I'm a great potato masher."

Early Thanksgiving morning, Buddy covered their red formica kitchen table with a white sheet. She set a place for Jane at the end opposite the Admiral, and she made sure all Jane's silverware had the same patterned handles.

From her grandmother's old recipe box, she took four blank but yellowed cards, folded them in half, and carefully wrote each of their names on one to mark their places at the table. In the center, where the turkey would go, she cut and laid a circle of sea grape branches, leaving a space just the right size for the platter.

She borrowed candle holders from Iris, then went back to see if she had any spare candles. She chose two used green ones, because they would look nice with the sea grape leaves, and burned the longer one until they were the same height.

Kirk was at the stove when Jane arrived. Though she parked near the kitchen door, Buddy went out the front to greet her and brought her in through the living room, then led her into the kitchen.

Jane smiled at Kirk and shook his hand, but when she saw the table, her place card, and the rose from Iris's garden on her plate, Jane's face went soft and tears welled in her eyes for a moment before she blinked them back. "Thank you," she whispered, and hugged Buddy. "I've never felt so welcome."

Kirk took the potato masher from a drawer and handed it to Jane. "I was told this is your specialty," he said, smiled, and jerked his thumb toward the pot on the stove. "Do a good job, the potatoes may be the only part of this meal we can chew."

"I'll get the Admiral," Buddy said, backing toward the door. She stopped when they turned to their jobs: Jane to the potatoes, Kirk to the cornbread, which was stuck to the pan. Buddy was still watching when Jane glanced at him in his struggle to bring even one chunk out whole. "Looks like it would be easier to cut the pan away," she said.

When her father laughed, Buddy released the fingers she had crossed behind her back, grinned, and left the kitchen.

"Well, will you look at this," the Admiral said, when Buddy wheeled him to his place.

She blushed.

"We ain't never eaten as fancy as this," he said, and winked at Jane.

"Now that we're all here," Jane said, "I have something for each of you." She went into the living room for the bag she'd left on a chair. From it she pulled a bottle of wine for Kirk, good wine, which she must have driven to Naples to buy. For the Admiral, she had framed the picture she'd taken of Buddy leaning over the railing at the Seaquarium, nose to nose with Hugo.

"And I brought this for you." She handed Buddy a soft, poorly wrapped package. "I thought it would match the skirt you wore to Miami."

Buddy opened it, carefully. The red V-necked cardigan was folded so the monogram, *EM*, in curly letters just below the left shoulder, was the first thing she saw.

Jane smiled at her. "It fits you now, Elizabeth Martin," she said.

Chapter 28

A week later, early on the day of her science report, Buddy went to the Admiral's door and rapped softly. When there was no answer, she opened it a crack and slid in. She still couldn't get used to the smell of tinkle in his stale, closed-up room. Before she woke him with his breakfast, she emptied the urinal, opened the blinds and the windows, and turned off the light on his dresser. When he said he wanted to hear her science report and would eat later, she collected every pillow in the house and packed them behind him, so he was sitting up like a real audience.

When she was done she closed her notebook.

"That was wonderful," the Admiral said and applauded by slapping the top of his nightstand. "I didn't know none of those things about stone crabs," he shifted one of the pillows, "and I been catching and eating 'em for sixty years."

"I'm still awful nervous, Admiral."

"I know, honey, that's natural, but I'm telling you, that

there will be the best report of any of 'em. You just wait. Now stand up and let me see how pretty you look." He made circles in the air with his finger.

She got out of his wheelchair and turned all the way around once. The skirt and blouse were the ones she had borrowed to wear to Miami. Over the blouse she wore her new red sweater.

Buddy faced the mirror on his dresser and straightened the long bow at her throat. With her index finger, she traced the initials on her sweater then turned, straightened her shoulders, lifted her chin high and grinned at her grandfather.

The Admiral took the picture Jane had given him of Buddy and Hugo from his nightstand and held it out, comparing them. "You're even prettier than this picture." He pressed it to his chest and shaded his eyes. "The room's glowing, you're so pretty."

"Oh, Admiral." She blushed.

He held his arms out to her. "Knock 'em dead, baby. Knock 'em dead."

Kirk siphoned most of the water in Osceola's tank into a bucket, then put the aquarium on the floor of the truck. He put the bucket in back and a coil of plastic tubing on the seat between them. Before starting the engine, he reached over and squeezed Buddy's shoulder. "You look beautiful," he said, and started the engine. When he turned to back out, he put his foot on the brake, reached and lifted her chin. "And I'm very, very proud of you."

Buddy leaned across the tubing to kiss his cheek.

Her father cleared his throat and took his foot off the brake. "Jane said she would like to sit in while you give your report. Do you mind?"

"I was hoping she could." Buddy smiled down at Osceola, then turned to grin at her reflection in the window.

After introducing Jane to the class, Ruth Daniels did as she had promised and called on Buddy, so she wouldn't have to sit and grow more nervous through other reports.

From her corner in the back, Buddy looked at Jane sitting in the little desk she'd dragged up beside Miss Daniels's. Her face was expressionless, but Buddy felt her eyes lift her, hold her steady, then balance her as she came slowly to the front of the room.

When she passed Alex's desk, he leaned over and whispered something to Jason. Muffled giggles erupted.

Buddy saw Jane's jaws tighten and her eyes narrow, but they did not leave Buddy's face.

At the corner of Miss Daniels's desk, still holding Jane's eyes, Buddy stopped and put her hand on the rim of Osceola's tank. As if dropping a safety line, she closed her eyes for a moment, took a deep breath, and turned to face the class. Sunlight poured in the high windows along the front wall, lighting Buddy's blonde head and warming her shoulders.

The children squirmed, grinning and whispering to each other, expectantly, like an audience before a performance. Miss Daniels's chair scraped back. The room grew quiet, except for Alex's last words to Timmy. "Dumb Buddy looks like a lit firecracker."

196

The class snickered.

Buddy's shoulders sagged and she lowered her head.

Jane's fingernail tapped the desktop. Buddy glanced at her and saw her straighten slowly in her desk and lift her head, chin held high. Buddy did the same.

"Elizabeth Martin on stone crabs," Miss Daniels announced, and sat down.

"My, my report is on stone crabs," Buddy whispered.

"A little louder," Miss Daniels said gently.

"My report is on stone crabs," Buddy repeated, her eyes cast down, her toes, bound in socks, working inside her sandals. "When stone crab eggs hatch, they don't look like baby crabs. They come out as little squiggly things that float in the water." She held up a drawing and pointed to the top figure. "These is—are called the lar . . . ." Buddy looked at the ceiling, not at Jane. "Larvae," she said suddenly. "These larvae keep changing shape." She drew her finger down the row of drawings. "Six times. These are called larvae stages. Larval stages," she corrected.

"The larvae float in on the tides and do their changing around the mangrove roots where they are food," she put the poster down, "for snook, trout," she ticked them off on her fingers, "redfish, mullet, jack, and grouper. Stone crab larvae is at the bottom of the food chain Miss Daniels told us about.

"Nothing eats full-growed crabs except octopuses and us. Conchs can get them when they are in a trap.

"To make sure stone crabs ain't extinct when we're growed, we need to protect the females with eggs, keep

197

the males out of the sun and wet when they are in the fish boxes, and be careful how we break the claws off.

"Osceola here had one claw snapped off at what Miss Conroy calls the . . . I've forgotten," she told the class and looked at Jane.

Jane nodded and turned to the class. "It's called the fracture plane. It's where the claw releases naturally without causing a wound."

"That's right," Buddy said. "His other claw was twisted off and his meat showed. If I hadn't kept my thumb over it, he'd have bled to death. Their blood ain't red," she added. "It's clear and sticky."

Buddy tapped the side of the tank. Osceola came to the end of the tube, looked up at her, then disappeared again.

"He's scared of everybody but me," she explained, pushed her sleeve up, reached in, tipped Osceola out, caught him as he scuttled across the tank, and held him up for them to see.

"The claw that got twisted off had to heal first." She tapped the left one. "So the little claws he's growing is different sizes. They're under this clear cover, so he can't pinch 'til he molts."

"Let me see," Belinda said.

Buddy, holding one hand under Osceola so he didn't drip on the floor, walked the aisles showing him to the ones who wanted to see. Alex looked away when she passed.

When she came around to Miss Daniels's desk, she carefully put him back in his tank. The class giggled when he scuttled across the sand, darted into the tube, crept back to the opening for a peek, then jerked himself out of sight.

Miss Daniels clapped her hands together. Jane joined in, as did all the children, except Alex, and Timmy after Alex hit him. "That was wonderful. Exactly what I wanted." She stood up. "Congratulations, honey," she said softly.

At lunch, Buddy put her tray down at the table with Naomi and Larry. Naomi smiled.

Belinda and Lisa, who were behind her in line, stopped as she was about to sit down. "Wouldn't you rather sit with us by the window with Megan and Pam?" Belinda asked.

"Sure. I . . . I guess so," Buddy stammered, stood up, then stopped. Naomi had lowered her head. Buddy sat down. "You go ahead," she said to Belinda. "I think I'll stay here."

The girls shrugged and walked away.

From the corner of her eye, Buddy saw Alex, Timmy, and Jason in a giggling knot, moving toward her. Alex stopped at the end of the table, grinned at her, then put his plate down and pushed it toward her.

For a moment Buddy couldn't face the truth of what he'd done. She couldn't look down, couldn't take her eyes off Alex's face. He was laughing so hard, tears ran down his cheeks.

"No, please, no," she whispered before she let her eyes

drop. The pain of the sight of Osceola dead was as sharp as a knife driven into her very soul. The noise of the children laughing and talking roared in her ears. She began to scream and scream, over and over, before finally lifting him to her cheek and rocking with him, gently.

She lifted her head only when Jane broke through the crowd. "Help me," she sobbed, lifting Osceola's steaming body up to her.

Jane shoved children aside, grabbed the crab out of Buddy's hand and poured someone's cold milk over the blisters on her palms, then pressed the cool, wet glass to the fiery print his shell had made on her cheek. "That son-of-a-bitch," she murmured, folding Buddy into her arms and rocking her. "That son-of-a-bitch."

Ruth Daniels dropped her hands away from her tear-streaked face and whirled on Alex, who tried to back away. No one behind him moved.

Buddy saw Coach Johnson snatch Alex out of Ruth Daniels's closing hands. Alex tried to squirm free of Mr. Johnson's grip. "If you don't hold still, I'll rip your arm off," Johnson snarled, jerking Alex.

Teachers began moving the children away. But the ones at the back, who hadn't seen what had happened, pushed in now to take a look. An eddy formed.

"There ain't nothing there but a stone crab," a little girl whispered to her friend. "Is she crying over that stone crab?"

"I think it was a pet."

"Got little claws, don't it?"

Alex had pried the shields off Osceola's new claws, broken them off and put them apart from the body, on the plate, with a catsup cap full of yellow mustard between them.

"You're hurting me," Alex whined, again trying to twist his arm free from Coach Johnson.

Buddy wiped her eyes, first on one shoulder then the other. She stood up, trembling like a muscle that's held a weight too long. "No more," she said to Alex. "No more." Her voice was soft and even. And like a pebble dropped in a pond, rings of silence swept across the cafeteria. "Don't ever call me dumb again. I'm not dumb. But if I was, there's nothing so dumb it ain't got feelings and can't be hurt." She put her hand over the shell of the crab.

"Osceola trusted me, knew I wouldn't hurt him. When you took him out of the tank and killed him, he was afraid. He died afraid . . ." Her voice cracked and tears ran down her cheeks. She lifted her head higher. "You shouldn't have killed Osceola," she said, then spread a napkin, placed his body in the center, laid his claws on top of his shell, folded the ends over, and put him in the pocket of her red plaid skirt.

She stepped over the bench and came around the table to face Alex. "I'm a better person than you, and I'm smarter."

Alex's eyes twinkled and a slight sneer twisted his lips.

"If nothing else, I'm bigger than you are." She squeezed her hand into a fist and swung at his face as hard as she could.

Alex's head snapped back and blood spurted from his nose. "She hit me," he wailed, covering his face. Blood dripped through his fingers. He lowered his hands, wiped them on his pants, and started to cry.

Jane drove her home.

"Admiral?" Buddy whispered from the doorway.

He was on his side, snoring softly.

The room was exactly as she'd left it just this morning: the blinds open, light off, wheelchair pulled close to the bed, one footrest up, one down, the way she'd left it when she got up to hug him good-bye. The only difference was he had put her picture back on the bedside table, beside the glass with his teeth. And the room smelled of tinkle again.

She stepped in, closed the door, and quietly slipped into his chair. "Admiral," she whispered. Tears slid down her cheeks. "Alex killed Osceola, Admiral." She reached above his head, took his Mack truck fishing cap off the bedpost, and put it on, then covered her face with her hands.

He sighed, turned on his back, and opened his eyes.

She straightened and pulled the cap lower.

"Is that you under there?"

"Yes, sir."

"Are you crying?"

"No, sir."

He leaned over trying to see under the brim.

She tilted her head up and smiled at him.

"Did the report go okay?"

"It was the best one."

"I told you, didn't I? How'd they like that crab?"

"I let him go, Admiral."

"Ah, that's what the sniffling's about." He patted her leg. "You think he was ready?"

"Yes, sir. He was ready."

"Don't feel bad, honey. It's the bravest love that gives freedom."

"Yes, sir. I had promised him."

"And he didn't look back, did he?"

"No, sir. Not once." She looked at the stain on the ceiling. "I'll miss him."

"I know, honey, but when something's born free, like your crab and them dolphins, then caught and kept, even by someone who loves and takes care of them, they still is only thinking about being free again."

"I never meant to keep him." Tears streaked her cheeks.

"Don't cry, honey." He took her hand. "He knows that now."

Before Jane left to go home, she and Buddy walked the road to Smallwood's. Buddy sat on the seawall, drew a circle in the sand by her left hip, then got on her knees and began to dig a hole. When it was deep enough, she lined it with the napkin, laid his claws in first then his body.

When she finished mounding the sand over Osceola, Buddy took her shoes and socks off, sat down, put her feet in the water, her arm around the piling and her cheek

against it. Jane came and sat beside her, the grave between them.

"How awful," Jane said of the pile of rusty engines.
"Such a pretty place to dump all that junk."

"Oh no, they ain't awful." Buddy smiled down at them.
"I like them and know who most of them belonged to."
She stretched her leg out until her big toe touched an exposed edge of one near the bottom of the pile. "This was
my great-grandfather's engine. Took Teddy Roosevelt tarpon fishing. And that one there," she pointed, "that was
the first school boat's motor. It used to drive Mr. Simmons crazy by quitting whenever it got around other engines. Putting it here was Mr. Simmons's revenge, but I
think it looks happy, don't you?"

Jane studied it, then shrugged.

"I like it here best when the tide is out and they stick out
of the water. Waves come in and fill them up and then go
out again, so it sounds like they're breathing. I want the
pitpan's motor to end here." She stroked the top of the
pile with her foot. "But I guess they ain't too pretty to
someone who don't know them."

"They're nicer than they were," Jane said.

Buddy ran her hand over the small mound of sand between them. "We all see things different, don't we?"

Jane nodded. "My mother used to say, there are three
hundred and sixty ways to see an elephant."

"She did? Why?"

"That was her way of saying what you just said. We all
see things differently. There are three hundred and sixty

204

degrees in a circle. If the elephant is in the center, everyone on the outside has a different view of him. See?"

"Yes 'am. I see." Buddy drew a circle around Osceola's grave, then looked at Jane. "It means as long as we is all looking at it from a different place, we ain't never gonna agree on what we see."

Jane put her arm around her and touched her forehead to Buddy's. "We can agree it's an elephant."

Buddy stood by the back door and waved as Jane pulled away. She had just turned to go in, when Jane honked, put the Volkswagen in reverse, backed back down the hill and stopped. She got out and walked to the railing. "This probably isn't the time, but I think you should know," she said gently, "Stevens lost his license; Marine Patrol will move the dolphins right after the holidays."

Buddy looked down and dug her toes into her sandals.

"I'm sorry, honey."

Buddy nodded.

"They will die if they are not moved. It's their only chance."

"I know."

A first quarter moon broke out of the clouds. Buddy looked up. Her cheeks glistened in its dim light. "Lucie has dolphin pox."

Jane winced and bit her bottom lip. "Does Annie?"

Buddy shook her head.

"It's not too late, honey."

Chapter 29

B<small>UDDY WAS CROSSING THE LIVING ROOM</small> when she heard her father swearing on the front porch. She tiptoed to the screen door.

He was on the first rung of a ladder, painting the porch ceiling. The plastic sheeting covering the porch was splattered with paint, as were his boots, pants, shoulders, and hair.

"Hi," she said. "Can I help?"

"May I . . .," he stopped, looked down at her and smiled. "I look like I need help, don't I?"

She grinned up at him and opened the screen door just wide enough to squeeze out onto the porch.

"Don't slip," he said, jerking his head to indicate a large circle of paint between the door and the ladder. "I hit the bucket with my elbow."

The ceiling was nearly done. Only an arc above the screen door was still the color of sanded-down green paint.

He looked down at her. "Jane tells me they are moving the dolphins."

Buddy nodded.

"I've been thinking, and I don't want you going up to see them anymore."

She bit her lip.

Kirk stepped down and opened the screen door. He dragged the ladder over and let the door flop against it. "It's going to be the crab thing all over again." He dipped the brush in the bucket of paint. "You'll be crushed when they move them to north Florida. And Stevens doesn't want you there."

"Annie does," Buddy said softly.

"The dolphin?" Kirk asked, scraping paint off the sides of the brush. He looked up smiling with amusement, but it disappeared when he saw her face. "Look," he said, laying the brush across the top of the can, "I just don't want you to be hurt again." He held his hand out to her. She came toward him and took it. "I want you to stop being hurt." His eyes narrowed and his voice became bitter. "By me, or anybody else."

"I already love Annie, so not seeing her again starting now would be as bad as not seeing her after they take her away."

Kirk sighed and nodded. "You win." Then he smiled. "Try not to get arrested, bail money is hard to come by."

"What's bail money?"

"When a dolphin lover gets thrown in jail, it's the money her father has to bring to get her out."

She grinned. "My piggy bank's on my dresser."

He laughed and stepped back up on the bottom rung of the ladder. "I'm almost done here," he said, "and I'm pulling traps tomorrow morning." He leaned down to check the lead-colored sky. "This front will stir the crabs up. So how about helping me do the railing tomorrow afternoon?"

"Sure."

"Good. I was looking for a sucker."

They smiled at each other, shyly, like new acquaintances.

Buddy came out on the porch after dinner, headed for Smallwood's to sit with Osceola and maybe to imagine Annie free somewhere in the bay, but it was raining. She crossed the slick, wet sheeting to the top step and stared at the dark, silent docks. A cold little wind was blowing from the northwest, rippling the puddles of water that had accumulated on the plastic covering. Buddy raised her chin, closed her eyes, and let raindrops streak her face. The cold drops seemed more right to her somehow than her own warm tears would have.

She sighed finally and turned to go in when her bare foot shot out from under her. She fell, spun on the sheeting, slid off the porch, and dropped onto the top step. It didn't hurt really, so she laughed. Then she remembered the sea lion at the Seaquarium. Buddy stepped back onto the porch, crossed to the far railing, did a short hop and slid the entire length of the porch with her arms out for balance.

~ ~ ~

The next morning, Buddy sat huddled on the milking stool in the stern of the pitpan. The rain the night before had preceded a cold front, which had left a crispness to the air, a biting, tingling coolness. She kept the bow into the wind until she reached the calm shoreline midway between the bridge and the mouth of Turner River, then she turned east. Out of the wind, it was warmer and the sky was cloudless and a deep blue.

She came out of the mangroves onto the river, then made the turn onto the prairie and saw the levee in the distance, looking like a narrow ribbon of dirt, an inch or two wide, hardly strong enough to trap and hold so much as the spirit of a dolphin.

Buddy thought of Hugo separated from his ocean by twenty-five hundred miles—and then of Annie, only ten miles from the sea. When the wind came from the south, Buddy bet that Annie and Lucie could smell their home, smell freedom.

At the north end of the levee, an airboat engine roared away from the dock. Buddy swerved off the open water into a stand of cattails and cut her motor. A limpkin screamed and lifted into the air like a question mark, its long neck and bill arcing, its thin legs hanging down. The airboat swept past her, its benches lined with tourists.

From her hiding place, she could see the roof of the chickee where gator hides were hung to dry. She left the cover of the cattails and poled toward it through yards of short sawgrass but out of sight of the ticket booth on the north end of the levee.

Willows lined the entire length of Stevens's property, except the trash dump. Behind the willows, on the high ground, was a wall of Florida holly. It looked impenetrable, but a horrible stench drew her to the narrow cleared path that led to the back of the chickee. Cast up in some willows branches, at the mouth of the trail, was Osceola's body, the skin shriveled and dry and wrinkled over his nearly rotted insides.

"This is as much as he cared," Buddy said angrily. "As little as you meant to him."

She tied the pitpan in the willows on the opposite side of the path from his body and waded up the trail. She came out behind the chickee just as a whistle blew and Stevens's voice announced the first trick to scattered applause.

The chickee was separated from the dolphin pond and the show pool by an open stretch of mowed weeds that ended at a stand of cattails. There were two splashes from the pool, some applause, then Stevens's voice announcing the next trick. Buddy moved silently off the path and along the edge of the holly. When she was opposite the bleachers, she bent low and tiptoed across to the cattails. The stand was too thick for her to see the water, but she could see the hoop held high by Stevens's son. The whistle blew. Annie sailed out of the water and through the hoop. Buddy grimaced and turned her face away. When the applause started, she clenched her hands into fists and covered her ears, pressing harder when Stevens called his son Arthur Murray and put on the Lone Ranger's theme.

When it was finally over and Annie and Lucie came through the gate between the pool and the pond, Buddy was waiting, standing knee-deep among the cattails. She squatted down and called softly to the dolphins. Annie saw her, veered and swept into the cattails next to Buddy's feet. When Buddy sat down and stretched her legs out straight, Annie lifted her head and laid it across her thighs. Buddy draped her arms across the dolphin's head and pressed her forehead to Annie's, just above her right eye. "They're gonna take you away," she said, breathing only in short gulps. She was trying not to cry. "It'll be a better place. The water's salt and there are other dolphins and . . . oh, Annie."

The airboat was returning.

Buddy sat up and wiped her eyes on her shoulders. "People can see me when they get off that boat." Annie lifted her head and Buddy scooted backward, deeper into the cattails. The dolphin lurched in beside her, flattening their cover. "Annie, they're gonna see us." She put her palm under Annie's snout, lifted it, and pulled some of the cattails free. Her fingers brushed across a small, hard, dry-feeling bump. Buddy clutched her stomach, dug her nails into her skin and rubbed the bump, before tilting Annie's head to see. It was white and cauliflower-shaped. Buddy threw her head back. "Not Annie," she sobbed. "Please, oh, please not Annie."

The airboat engine whirred and died.

211

Crying softly, she laid back in the water, deep enough to cover her ears. Annie pressed her snout to Buddy's cheek where the scalded patch of skin was peeling. Though the burn itself no longer hurt, it was a pressure—Annie's skin on hers—that she could not stand. Buddy moved her face away, and thought of stone crabs, remembered that when their shells become too small, tighten around them, give them no more room, no peace, they empty themselves of water, and shrivel down until they can escape. That's what she wanted to do, to empty out, shrink until she could escape her skin, now tight and cracked. She felt as if her shell had failed her, broken open, and let the belief that nothing she loved could die slip out.

Annie shifted so her snout again bumped Buddy's cheek.

"Oh, Annie, if you could only understand me," Buddy cried, in frustration. "A dolphin at Seaquarium jumped twenty-three feet. All that's keeping you in here is ten feet of dirt. I can't believe you couldn't jump right across that levee if only you knew you could." Buddy rolled over to face Annie. "If I could just explain it to you."

Annie jerked her head, whistled softly, and nudged her.

"I don't want to play, Annie. I feel too bad."

Stevens was into his long-winded sales pitch again. It had been a numbing noise chopping up the stillness like white caps. When it ended, she raised her head and looked across the pond. The airboat's engine fired up. Stevens hung the microphone on a hook inside the ticket booth and waved as the airboat pulled away from the dock. The driver tested the rudders, blasting Stevens and rocking him back a few steps. In Buddy's mind, it toppled him and drove him on his butt across the parking lot and out onto the highway where a semi rolled over him. She had a wistful look when she dipped her hand and splashed water onto Annie's drying skin. It became slick and slippery again. Buddy ran her hand along her side, glanced at Stevens, waddling toward the gift shop, then scooped more water over Annie. "I've got an idea," she said suddenly, getting on her knees and splashing more and more water on the dolphin. "I've got an idea." She kissed Annie's forehead. "I'll be back the night of the full moon."

Chapter 30

AT HOME THAT EVENING, Buddy sat beside her grandfather's bed in his wheelchair.

"I don't see it as stealing," he said. "The state's already decided he ain't doing right by them. All you're planning is to move them early and to a different location." He ducked his head to see into her eyes, smiled and squeezed her hand. "My little girl," he whispered. "I'll miss my little girl."

"I ain't ever leaving you, Admiral."

"I know that. I mean if you get your dolphins out, you will come back all growed up."

She leaned and put her arms around his neck. "I'd still be your little girl." His lips were dry against her forehead and his breath was warm.

"That ain't the way it's suppose to be. To keep you my little girl would be as wrong as penning them dolphins." He stroked her forehead then lifted her chin. "I've never seen such a love of something like you got for that dolphin. If she's sick with what killed the male, you have to try to do this, honey. And if you succeed, you'll do all your growing when she swims out of the reach of your hand. You'll want her to stay because you love her and you'll want her to go because you love her." He put his head back on the pillow and closed his eyes. "I always thought I'd die at sea—pull a trap full of crabs or a net full of fish and just keel over. But here I am, like them dolphins, trapped, legless, yards from the sea, and no way to get there." He turned and looked at her, tears ran down the gullies in his face. "Show her the way home, honey. Show her for me."

Chapter 31

A WEEK LATER, Buddy lined her pillows up under her blanket and took her cap from the bedpost. She crossed the hall to her grandfather's door. Moonlight glowed through the venetian blinds, casting bars across his bed and the floor and his wheelchair. He snored softly.

"I'm going now," she whispered, then snapped her fingers, spun, and ran on tiptoes to her room. From the top drawer of her dresser, she got the purse she'd carried to Miami. It held the ticket stub from the Seaquarium and the Admiral's eyetooth, which she took and put in the pocket of her jeans. Before she left she adjusted her blinds so no light fell on her bed, then tiptoed to her father's door and pressed her ear against the thick wood. He, too, snored softly.

At her grandfather's door, she stood for a moment and watched the bedcovers rise and fall with each breath.

"I got your tooth, Admiral," she whispered, patted her pocket, then silently closed his door and pressed her forehead to its wood. "So you can keep an eye on me."

It was ten to eleven by the clock on the stove. She took a flashlight from the drawer next to the refrigerator, slipped out the kitchen door and around to the shed. Without using the light, she felt around in the corner until her hand hit what was left of the roll of plastic sheeting. She lifted it onto her shoulder.

The docks were lit by one bright light near the cleaning stand. Buddy crossed through Iris's backyard, staying in the shadows until she was opposite her father's dock slip, then she darted across. She boarded his boat on the port side from the seawall, crossed to the pitpan, and dropped the sheeting onto the deck. From the trunk cabin of her father's boat, she got a bucket and a tow rope.

Sitting on her knees in the bow, she paddled the pitpan away from the docks, out of the channel, and along the shore until she was opposite Smallwood's silent, dark store. To her ears in the still night, the little motor, when she started it, sounded as loud as an airboat engine.

Once away from the island, the bay was a flat calm, and as silvery as a new baking sheet. The pitpan's wake sliced it into two halves. Twice, schools of mullet exploded out of the water in front of the bow in a shower of phosphorescence. At the mouth of the river, her approach disturbed a roost of ibis. They rose into the air in a thunderous squawking protest.

It was bright where the river was wide and open, but where it narrowed and the mangroves on either side joined their limbs in a dense tangle above her head, it was very dark. Red eyes appeared, then amid a rustle of leaves and the creak and sway of branches, disappeared.

"Raccoons," she said aloud, hopefully. She did not use the flashlight, afraid that when and if she really needed it, the batteries would be dead.

Spider webs, easily ducked in the day, stretched unseen across the black tunnel and ripped away when her face went through them. As she came out of the tunnel, onto the river, she took down a web that left a large golden orb spider dangling off the bill of her cap. She lifted the cap by the button on the crown, lowered it until the spider got its footing on a gunnel, then she broke the strand that linked them and put the cap back on her head.

Stevens's levee looked like a narrow white scar on the pale face of the prairie. A hundred yards short of it, a distance she hoped was far from anyone's hearing, she cut the pitpan's motor. When the engine went silent so did the frogs, leaving absolute stillness.

Buddy, who was nearly always alone, felt suddenly mired in loneliness. She wadded the tooth pocket in her fist and looked up at the moon, now very high, its face dim and far away.

As if on some signal, a gator grunted far off to her right, and the frogs, as one, began to croak again. Before she could feel grateful, the scream of a frog, like that of a woman, silenced the others. She shuddered. "A gator got it," she said, just to hear a human voice.

She poled the rest of the way, tied the bow up in the willows, and jammed the pole in the mud for the stern line. She threw the roll of sheeting up on the levee, then stepped out and up the embankment with the bucket.

The levee had been formed out of the rock and sediment removed to make the pond. On the river side, the wash of airboat wakes had created a sharp, foot-high lip, while the pond side sloped gently to the water's edge then dropped off abruptly into the deep, murky water.

Buddy chose what looked like the narrowest point that was still a safe distance from the parking lot and the lights of the occasional car and semi. She cleared the path to the river of any large rocks then unrolled the plastic.

Unfolded, it was a good four feet wide and long enough to reach the water on both sides. Buddy dipped the bucket in the river and splashed it across the sheeting. The moon came into focus on the plastic and shone up at her. She bit her lip, glanced skyward with her palms pressed together, then hopped and slid from the river to a point three feet from the edge of the levee. It was there she lost her footing, spun a half turn and slid the rest of the way on her fanny, then down the slope backward and sank into the pond.

Annie pushed her head against Buddy's stomach and lifted her onto the shallow slope. She upended and whistled through her blowhole, then spun in a circle, throwing water in an arc with her flippers before pushing up beside Buddy and opening her mouth.

Buddy tickled her tongue, bent and kissed her forehead. "I'm gonna get you, and Lucie, too, if I can, out of here." She stood and stepped up on the levee. Annie squeaked, slid back in the water, and bobbed her head as if she were all for it.

"Shh." Buddy put a finger to her lips.

She filled the bucket again and again, wetting the plastic until it was a glistening silver trail.

"Watch me, Annie." Buddy skipped, slid toward the river, then ran back to the pond. "Come to me." She bent and patted her thighs, then knelt and ran her hand back and forth across the sheeting. "Come up here with me." She backed away, toward the river. "Come on, girl."

Annie made two small circles then stood upright on her tail, clicked and squealed.

"Please, Annie, try."

The dolphin dove and came up in the center of the pond.

"Come on, girl." Buddy walked backward, patting her thighs.

The dolphin disappeared. A moment later, she was beside Buddy on the levee.

Buddy pressed her hands against Annie and put her weight into trying to push her farther before she realized Annie had gone as far as she was going.

Buddy covered her eyes with her hands and sank to her knees on the sheeting beside the dolphin.

Annie had come to a stop with her head almost dead center on the levee. Her flukes hung out over the pond. She arched her back and swung her tail, trying to move. The effort skidded her sideways toward the edge of the sheeting.

"Don't, Annie," Buddy cried, pushing against her. "Don't get on the gravel. I'll get you across."

Buddy straddled Annie's head and tried to pull her forward by her dorsal fin. Annie pumped her tail in the air above the water. It was an attempt good only in inches. Buddy got the bucket and poured water over Annie and around her on the sheeting, then got in front of her and tried again until she lost her footing and threw herself sideways to keep from landing on the dolphin's head. She did not feel the gravel tear her skin.

"Don't move, Annie. I've got a rope. I'll pull you over with the pitpan."

Lucie was upright a few feet behind Annie's tail, clicking and whistling. When Buddy came back up the bank with the rope, Lucie sank into the black water.

It wasn't until she was there with the rope that Buddy realized there was no way to get it past the point where Annie's neck rested on the levee. She flung the rope to the ground, jumped off into the water, and tried to pull her back into the pond by her tail.

Annie turned her head and rolled a little sideways to watch, but otherwise did not move.

Lucie squealed and ran herself up onto the shallow shelf, a few yards down from where Buddy was trying to pull Annie back into the water.

Annie answered, as if she, too, was frightened.

Buddy scrambled up, grabbed the rope, looped it around Annie's tail and knotted it. "Lucie, come help us," she called. She waded in and swam out with the rope. "See, like this." She held it up for Lucie to see and pulled it tight. "Pull Annie back in." She swam slowly toward Lucie with the rope in her teeth. The dolphin clicked frantically, jerked her head sharply, and was gone.

Buddy dropped the rope, swam to the shelf, crawled up beside Annie and lay beside her on the sheeting. The moon, high and small, was straight overhead. "I don't know what else to do, Admiral," she said, then rolled and put her arm across the dolphin's head and her cheek next to Annie's.

In the pond, Lucie stood on her tail, watching, clicking.

Buddy, as she had so many times in the week since she'd found him, thought of Osceola's body out back in the weeds. Buddy suddenly gasped and sat up. As clearly as a nightmare come true, she had pictured Annie there with him, her skin empty and shriveled, her huge heart silent and still.

She struggled to her feet. A dim circle had formed around the moon, like it got sometimes before a rain. She looked out across the prairie and realized it was brighter than it had been coming, as if the circle was a mirror reflecting a candle. And though she hadn't noticed it before, the river ran like a silver trail as far as she could see. "I'm going home for help, Annie."

She poured bucket after bucket of water over the dolphin. "I'm going home for help," she said again, then stepped into the pitpan, untied the stern line, and loosened the bowline. She refilled the bucket. "Please don't move. Please understand me." She emptied the bucket over Annie, then ran and jumped down into the pitpan, started the engine and jerked the last line loose from the willows. Glancing back over her shoulder, she saw Annie lift her head and heard her frightened whistle, even above the noise of the engine.

She approached the point where the airboat trail enters the river too fast. She swept sharply right, but the stern slid into the shallows. The prop caught in the mud and stopped. She tried over and over to start the motor, but it was too muddy and clogged with weeds. She grabbed the pole and frantically pushed the stern free, then stepped to the bow and poled toward deeper water, jamming it in hard over and over. She hit something solid. *Limestone,* she thought, in the instant before the bow of the pitpan rose out of the water, tipped up on one side, and threw her out. The moment she went over, she knew she'd hit a gator—a big gator. She came straight out of the water, she believed without ever touching bottom, and flung herself over the side into the boat. There was a wide swatch of flattened sawgrass where the startled gator had shot out from under the pitpan. His wake still rippled away, swaying the grass in the moonlight.

Shivering as much from the cold as her fright, Buddy got the flashlight and shone it in a circle around the pitpan for the pole. It was yards away in an open area among some lily pads. She got the paddle and pulled herself toward it. She was nearly there when a dark form broke the surface near it. She flicked the light on and aimed it at the black, bumpy mass. The gator sank slowly. His eyes glowed red on the surface for a moment, then disappeared. She turned the pitpan and eased it between the pole and where she had last seen the gator, then hunkered in the bow and waited. When he did not come up, she slowly lifted an oar and brought it down sharply against the bow. The gator spun away beneath the surface, rocking the boat. Buddy snatched the pole.

Chapter 32

BUDDY WENT UP THE WHEELCHAIR RAMP at a dead run. She stopped herself against the back railing, jerked the kitchen door open, and bashed through the swinging door into the living room. She hit her father's door with a thud and flung herself at him.

He bolted straight up. "Jesus, what is it?" He grabbed her shoulders. "What's wrong?"

"Annie's stuck on the levee."

"What?"

"Annie—my dolphin—she's stuck on the levee."

"Damn it." He leapt up, pulled on the jeans he'd thrown over the chair, and ran with her through the house.

"How did this happen?" he asked, jerking open the truck's door.

Buddy had stopped behind the truck. "We need the pit-pan."

"What for?" He came around and stood staring down at her.

Buddy hesitated. For the first time she felt how really cold and wet she was. "If we get Annie across, I'm taking her out to the Gulf."

"Oh no you're not."

"Yes, sir. I am." She straightened her shoulders and looked up at him. "Daddy, she and Lucie both have the same thing that killed Osceola." She blinked back tears. "Moving them to some place like the Seaquarium won't help. The only difference between their pools and Stevens's hole in the ground is the water's cleaner. I don't want her to die in a fish tank."

"You can't be sure she'll die, besides, it's stealing," he said lamely.

"No, sir. It's not. Mr. Blossom's the one that done the stealing. He stole Annie and Lucie and Osceola, just the same as colored people got stolen from Africa. I'm not stealing, I'm showing them the way back home."

Kirk took her hand, and though his face was full of regret, he said, "I can't help you do that. They still belong to him for another two weeks."

Buddy jerked her hand free, turned and ran down the road to the boat ramp. Jane was the only person left. As she untied the pitpan, she heard her father start the truck and the gravel crunch as he backed toward her.

He set the emergency brake, got out, walked to the back and dropped the tailgate. "I guess . . .," he said, as he came down the ramp for the pitpan, "that it boils down to how you see things. I'm not sure you are right, but I'm less sure that I am. Maybe you're teaching me that the fine line in between is the most we can hope for." When she was in the truck, he closed the door on her side then hesitated at her window. "I do know . . ." He touched her cheek. ". . . without a doubt, you deserve more for a father than you've got."

With the pitpan in the bed of the truck, Kirk and Buddy tore up the highway and skidded into the Everglade Eden parking lot. Buddy leapt out and ran to the levee. There, in the moonlight, right where she had left her, lay Annie. The dolphin lifted her head and whistled a greeting.

Buddy jumped the chain and ran to her. She filled the bucket and poured it over Annie, then dropped to her knees beside her. "That's my dad, but don't be afraid. He ain't like he was in September."

Buddy motioned for her father to come on, slowly. She spoke softly to the dolphin, reassuringly, as her father came down the levee toward them. Annie watched his progress with her eyes rolled, but she stayed quiet.

"Put your hand out," Buddy whispered. "If she doesn't act scared, touch her."

Kirk did as he was told and slowly moved his hand toward the dolphin. Annie lifted her head and tail, as if in preparation to swim away.

"It's all right, Annie." Buddy stroked the dolphin's forehead, then took her father's hand and held it for Annie to see. She placed it against Annie's side, then slid her own out leaving his against the dolphin's skin.

Kirk smiled a smile of discovery. "She feels like a wet inner tube."

Annie lowered her tail and head. When Kirk's hand

227

crossed her blowhole, she squeezed a little jet of air through causing him to jerk his hand away. He laughed. "An inner tube with a sense of humor."

"Yeah." Buddy smiled. "She likes to tease."

Buddy poured water over and around Annie, then took the rope off her tail. "I want to pull her back into the pond."

"Why not just across into the river?" Kirk asked.

"Because if she doesn't slide across on her own, she won't know what to tell Lucie."

When he shrugged, she could tell he didn't believe Annie could do that. Buddy wasn't sure of it herself.

Kirk got on one side of her tail and Buddy on the other. They each braced a foot against the edge of the levee. "On three," Buddy whispered. "Ready, Annie?"

The dolphin turned a little to look at her, then straightened and lay still.

"I think she understood you," Kirk said.

"I hope she did. Ready?" she asked. "One, two, three."

For a moment, as hard as they pulled, nothing happened, then slowly Annie began to move backward across the sheeting. When her middle was off the edge, Buddy let go. "She'll do the rest," she told her father.

When he was clear, Annie whipped her tail in circles, cocked herself sideways, teetered for a second, and fell into the water.

Lucie swept by and Annie shot off with her toward the end of the pond. A moment later, they came speeding back. Annie veered off and circled toward Buddy, who waded out to her.

"Will you try again, Annie?" Buddy asked, stroking her. Annie upended and bobbed her head.

"I don't believe that," Kirk muttered and sat down on the side of the levee with his feet in the water.

Annie let out a series of clicks, flopped sideways, and disappeared. A second later, she rose out of the water and did a somersault in the air.

"Bet Ole Orange Blossom didn't know she could do that," Kirk said.

"He ain't ever gonna know, either." Buddy grinned.

Her father helped her straighten the sheeting, then passed up bucket after bucket of water until it was completely wet and glistening in the sinking moonlight. Before Buddy went to the edge of the levee to call Annie, Kirk moved down into the shadow of the ticket booth.

Annie came across the pond, popped up at the end of the plastic carpet and squeezed a long, shrill whistle out of her blowhole.

Buddy patted the tooth in her pocket then crossed her fingers. "Come with me, girl." She pounded her thighs, then turned and ran the length of the sheeting to the river. "Come on, Annie," she called.

Annie flung herself sideways and dove.

For a second, the pond where she had been, flattened like a scar, then a breeze rippled it, removing any trace. A moment later Buddy saw the water hump like a mole's trail in a garden, then Annie was on the levee. Buddy leapt clear of the sheeting as she swept past and broke the silvered surface of Turner River's black water.

Kirk's fist shot into the air.

229

Buddy jumped straight into the river.

Annie made a sweeping circle of the deep channel, upended in front of Buddy, twirled and twirled, spraying water in an arc, then flopped sideways and disappeared.

Kirk laughed and pointed toward a trail of flattened sawgrass. "Your dolphin scared the devil out of that big sucker," he said, of the gator barreling away in the opposite direction.

Buddy, treading water, turned looking for Annie. A fin came up behind her and slid into her hand. She took it and felt Annie buck beneath the surface to gain speed. Annie dragged her around the channel, faster and faster until the water churned and Stevens's airboats scraped and crashed against each other.

Buddy dropped off when they were opposite the sheeting.

Her dad was sitting cross-legged on the levee—smiling.

Annie circled and swam back to her. "No more, Annie, we have to go." To her father, she said: "Keep down so Lucie can't see you, okay?"

He got up, walked out on the dock, and took a seat on the edge with his feet in the water.

Buddy put her arm across Annie's back. "Call Lucie," she said.

Lucie was frantic on the other side. She had been clicking and whistling. Now, for the first time, Annie answered.

Buddy swam and heaved herself over the side of the pitpan, pulled its bow into the willows, then parted them so she could see the pond. "Call her now, Annie. Make her come with us."

On one side of the levee, Annie circled, clicking, whistling, and squeaking. On the other, Lucie did the same. Annie's calls had an excited tone; Lucie's sounded distressed. Annie leapt into the air. Lucie did the same. The second time they jumped, it was at the same time. They saw each other for a moment. When Annie came up again, she stood on her tail at the end of the sheeting and began to click, slowly, with a beat between each one. Lucie swam in slow circles on her side, then stood upright a little to the left of the sheeting. She seemed to listen, but made no sound before she sank away and came up where the plastic floated on the surface. She butted it with her snout, then propelled herself forward until her head rested on it.

"Keep calling, Annie," Buddy whispered.

Annie clicked, fell backward, circled and leapt in the air. Lucie answered, pushed herself off the sheeting, made a sweeping circle of their pond and disappeared.

Buddy glanced at her father. He was sitting very tall with his neck stretched. She signaled him with her hand to get down.

Annie appeared to do as her father was told and sank from sight.

Buddy gnawed at her bottom lip and scanned the choppy surface of the river looking for a fin. "There isn't much time left, Annie," she whispered. "Where are you?"

Lucie pushed back up on the sheeting and lay quietly. A

sudden stillness came. The frogs stopped croaking, the airboats had ceased bumping each other, and the breeze had died. Miles away, from the intersection of the highways, Buddy heard the gears of a semi shifting as it gained speed after turning onto 41 from the road to Immokolee. She glanced at the road then back at the river. Annie was on the far side, shadowy against the sawgrass. She squeezed one long, shrill note out. Lucie gave one pump of her tail and splashed back into the water. Annie sank just below the surface and started clicking. It was a constant even series of sounds. Buddy's heart began to pound. "This is it," she whispered. Her father nodded and gave her a thumbs-up.

The rumble of the approaching semi drowned out Annie's signals. The arc of its headlights swept across her father. Buddy grimaced and squeezed her eyes shut for a moment. When she opened them, Lucie was on the levee, in a slow slide, out of sync with the sweeping roar of the semi. She came to rest on the edge, her head above the river, her flippers inches short of the lip of the levee. Annie came up and pressed her face to Lucie's.

Her father started to get up.

"Wait," Buddy said. "If she gets scared and rocks herself off the plastic, we'll never get her in." She sat on the gunnel of the pitpan then dropped into the water.

Lucie watched her; the eye Buddy could see rolled sharply back in her head, her body stiff, tail lifted. Buddy spoke softly, swam slowly. Lucie did not move.

When Buddy reached her, she lifted her hand and

touched Lucie's cheek, stroked it gently. Lucie arched her back slightly then lowered her tail.

"All right," Buddy said to her father without looking at him. "Come slowly."

When he got up, Lucie's head jerked in his direction and she began to click frantically. Her tail whipped in the air and her flippers slapped the sheeting.

"Lucie, stop," Buddy cried.

But the dolphin's eyes were round in panic. She made a noise that sounded like whop, whop, whop and beat her flukes against the sheeting, trying to swim away. The thrashing propelled her forward the few inches it took for her flippers to hit the sides of the levee. It crumbled a little beneath her. She threw her head up, then down, whipped her tail in a circle, and pitched into the river.

"All right!" Kirk whooped and slapped his thigh.

Buddy grinned, scampered up the side of the levee and launched herself into her father's arms.

He picked her up and swung her around, hugged her, then held her out straight like a wet, dripping rag doll. The print of her thin body marked his shirt and pants. Kirk put her down, but held one of her shoulders and lifted her face by her chin, then he, too, looked straight up. "Did you see that, Elizabeth. Did you see our wonderful daughter?"

The eastern sky was graying.

Her father bent and kissed her cheek. "Take your dolphins home, baby," he said, and started toward the truck.

"Do you want to come with us?"

Kirk stopped and turned. "Do you still need me?"

Buddy looked down at her feet. "I just think we should finish this together."

He came back and took her hand.

Buddy had not realized how shallow and muddy the airboat trail through the prairie was until Annie balked at leaving the deep water of the river. She started into it, churned the deep mud with her tail, stopped and backed off. Buddy tried to reassure her, stood and called her, but she lay still, clicking.

The alligator she had jabbed hours ago flickered briefly in her mind before she went over the side and waded, armpit deep, through the muck to Annie. She bent and stroked her snout, spoke softly, then waded with the dolphins the length of the trail to where the river deepened again for its trip through the mangroves.

Her father followed at a distance in the pitpan and waited while Buddy swam with the dolphins to rinse the mud off. His eyes were sad when he lifted her back into the boat, but "I've missed so much" was all he said.

The sky was just turning pink by the time they reached the mangrove tunnel. When they came out the other end, the pink glow had crept across the horizon. "It's a dolphin sky," Buddy said, and smiled. "Pink on the bottom and gray on the top."

The river opened up and the tide tugged, pulling them gently downstream. When they reached the subtle stretch of the river where it shifts between brackish and fresh with the tides, the dolphins sped around the pitpan, taking the lead for a few yards, then dropping back, as if unsure. Annie made large, fast, sweeping circles, slowing at the bottom of each arc to slide close to the boat, turn on her side, part her jaws in a deep smile, then shoot away again.

As they rounded the last bend of the river, the first whitecaps of the bay were visible. "There's your home, Annie," Buddy said.

Lucie had gone way ahead, but Annie came back again and again to circle and nudge the pitpan, bumping it with her snout.

"I'm going as fast as I can," Buddy told her when she stood on her tail and waited for them to catch up.

"What's the other one doing?" her father asked, pointing to where Lucie floated with her back arched high out of the water.

Buddy steered toward her, but the dolphin moved away. She shaded her eyes with her hands and squinted against the reflected light on the water.

Annie zipped past Lucie, then swam back and made slow circles around her. After a few moments, Lucie straightened and began to move again toward the open sea.

Buddy followed, keeping the pitpan against the eastern wall of mangroves, away from Chokoloskee. The dolphins stayed out in front, but on the course she had set.

"How far are you taking them?" Kirk asked. He was sitting in the bow on the milking stool with his long legs drawn up like a frog.

"To where there ain't a speck of mud in the water."

Beyond the mangrove islands, out of Rabbit Key Pass, the water turned from pale brown to pale green, then to blue. A hundred yards in front of the pitpan, just where the water turned the deepest blue, Annie and Lucie soared into the air, side by side. Two dolphins—with three tails.

They looked at each other. "What was that?" Kirk asked.

Buddy stared, blinked as if to clear her vision, then grinned suddenly. "Lucie's having her baby," she whooped, and threw her arms around her father's neck. "We brought back the exact number he stole."

For less than an hour, Lucie floated quietly in the water, her back arched, tail down. Annie floated between the pitpan and Lucie. Buddy stroked her with one hand and held her father's with the other.

When Lucie raised her tail, their hands tightened. When the water turned brown beneath her, her father kissed the side of her face.

Lucie dove. Annie followed.

A moment later, they surfaced again. The baby, draped across its mother's snout, opened its blowhole and filled its lungs with its first breath of air—air heavy only with the smell of the sea, not garbage or rotting fish or the sound of traffic. Lucie rolled on her side and looked at Buddy. Her baby bumped her with its snout then swung around and rested at its mother's side. Lucie drifted toward the pitpan until the baby was an arm's length away. Buddy slowly reached out until her fingers touched the tip of its dorsal fin. Lucie lifted her head, gave one long whistle, then, with a pump of her tail, took her baby toward the open sea.

Annie followed them for a few yards then came back. Buddy bit her lip. "Balance me, please," she said to her father.

Kirk leaned a little starboard while she swung her legs over the port side, kicked, and dropped off into the water. Annie glided up beside her and stood on her tail.

Buddy reached up and put her thumb over the dry white bump on the underside of Annie's snout. The thumb that had sealed Osceola's wound and saved his life, for a time. She wrapped her other arm around the dolphin and laid her head against the pink folds of her neck. Annie's flippers were under her arms.

"It's okay, Annie," Buddy said softly. "You should go with Lucie. That's where you belong, where you have always belonged." Tears came and Buddy could not stop them. Against her legs she could feel Annie's tail move gently, keeping them afloat. "When I miss you," she said, "I'll close my eyes and remember how much I loved you and how you loved me." She pressed her face to the dolphin's neck and closed her eyes. "I can still see you, Annie," she whispered, then let her arms float open.

Annie lowered her head, touched her snout to Buddy's ear, then sank away without a sound.

Buddy groped behind her for the side of the pitpan, turned and pressed her forehead to the gunnel. "That's my girl," she heard the Admiral whisper. "We're free now, baby. We're all free now."

Her father put his hands under her arms, where Annie's

flippers had just held her, lifted her into the boat and wrapped his arms around her. "She'll come back," he said.

"I don't think so, Daddy." With her head against his shoulder, she turned to face the sea. "I don't think I'll ever know where she is, but I'll know where she ain't."

Epilogue

BUDDY MARTIN, three months and one week into her twelfth year, sat on the seawall beneath Smallwood's store and watched the water move like a cold breath back and forth across her long, tanned feet. She hooked her right arm around a piling and, with her left index finger, drew circles around the small mound of sand beside her. She divided the wait for him between watching the horizon and the circles she drew.

She stopped finally, wiped her sandy finger on her overalls, sighed, and closed her fist around the tooth in her pocket. She put her cheek against the wood and shut her eyes.

For an hour she waited like that, eyes closed, cheek against the piling. There was no sound, no breeze, only her toes felt touched by life as the cold water seeped in, seeped out, until she became aware that the blackness behind her lids had lightened.

She opened her eyes. "Admiral?"

Just above a mangrove island, as if seated in its branches, rested the full moon. Its pale, ancient face smiled at her.

"Is that you there, Admiral? I've been waiting," she whispered.

THE END

Glossary

by Elizabeth "Buddy" Martin

I was thinking how hard it was for me to read, much less figure out, what every one of them words meant and that you might have trouble with some of them yourself. I made a list of the ones that might trip you up and defined them the best I could. 'Course, just about everything I know, the Admiral taught me. I guess I'll always be seeing the world through his eyes.

I know lots of folks ain't ever seen an *airboat*. I still ain't never rode in one, and I live here. The Admiral hated them 'cause of the noise, but I'd kind of like to see for myself. Guess that don't help you figure out what they look like, does it?

They're made of aluminum and flat as a skillet on the bottom 'cause they're only used in real shallow water, like the sawgrass prairie. They can go just about anywhere in the Everglades, even across dry land with a good head start, 'cause instead of a prop underwater to get snagged on stuff, it's got an airplane propeller mounted on the stern, which blows the boat across the water. The driver steers it with a stick that controls the rudders. A little push one way or the other changes the direction the rudders is pointing, which shifts the wind the propeller is making and blows you off in another direction. They can about turn on a dime. I've seen 'em do it.

The driver's seat is real tall, like a baby's high chair, so the driver can see where he is going. It's attached to the big wire cage around the engine, which is there to keep the driver from getting some part of himself lopped off.

Stevens's airboat rides were along trails through the prairie where the sawgrass had been beat back from the constant traffic. But anyone cutting through dense prairie that ain't sitting up high comes out looking like he's been paper-cut from stem to stern.

If you was to open a tin can at both ends and toss the lid and the bottom away, you'd have yourself the spitting image of a *bait chute.* You need one big enough to shove a fish head through, but anything real smelly is about all that's needed to get the attention of a crab.

In rough seas or a good hard rain, a boat takes on a lot of water. Most of it runs off the deck through holes in the sides of the boat called *scuppers,* but some is always getting below deck with the engine. Without a *bilge pump* to pump that water out, you'd pretty soon find yourself on the bottom, watching the crabs coming for you.

In English, we got so many words spelled just alike but don't sound alike and ain't even related. *Bow* is one. You can "tie a bow" or "take a bow." *Bowline* sounds like the take-a-bow one, but it's the rope on the front end of a boat that you use to tie it up. Don't that take all?

To connect Chokoloskee to the rest of Florida, they built a *causeway*. It ain't nothing more than piled-up oyster shells and mud they dug out of the bay. When they had a high, dry strip long enough to reach from the island to Everglades City, they paved it. The Admiral loved when storm waves washed over the causeway, 'cause it cut the tourists off. He said if they'd built a bridge instead, we'd never get a break from people wanting to come here and rough it for a day or two.

The Admiral says that the Indians is the only ones who build real *chickees*. There must be a secret to 'em that I don't know. They is only four pine or cypress posts and layers of palm fronds for a roof. I guess it's how they layer the fronds, 'cause I ain't never been in one that leaked in the rain, and they're sure shady and cool in the summer.

The first time I heard about those metal pointy things on the bottom of football players' shoes called cleats, I was really confused. A *cleat* to me is that two-armed metal thing on a dock that you tie a bow- or a stern line to. They don't look nothing like the bottom of a shoe.

Don't *cowling* sound like what you'd call a baby cow? It ain't, of course. It's the cover over an engine to keep rain and dirt out.

A *culvert* ain't nothing but a big concrete or metal pipe stuck through from one side to the other of a road across water or a levee to let the water through. If they hadn't built the levee, they wouldn't need a culvert.

A *dory* is a boat about twice as big as the pitpan but just as flat on the bottom. The pitpan has real low sides, and the dory's are high and flare out. It has a bigger engine and will take a lot rougher water, but I'm happy with a pitpan, though I don't use it as much as I used to.

An *eddy* is like an underwater tornado, a whirlpool. Don't tell nobody I suggested this, but watch next time you flush your toilet . . . that there's an eddy.

The Admiral once told me that north of the equator the water rushes around one way, and goes the opposite direction south of the equator.

Miss Conroy's the one who explained all about *estuaries* to me. Seems that in most places where rivers flow into the sea, they get kind of wide and shallow, and this is where the flow of the river mixes up with the tides. That's what most estuaries look like. The mouth of Turner River is an estuary like that. But Miss Conroy said that our whole coast from the west side of the Keys to over near Naples is an estuary because the Everglades is nothing

244

but one big river emptying into the Gulf. Turner River looks more like the rivers other people picture, but it ain't bound up with dry land on either side. It's just got water too deep for mangroves to take root in.

A *gunnel* is also called a gunwale. I don't know why they need two names for the same thing; spelling one is hard enough. Anyway, a gunnel is just the strip of wood that caps the sides of boats. On big boats like my dad's, it's wide enough to walk along if you got something to hold on to.

Our house on Chokoloskee faces southeast, which is the windward side of the island most of the year. In the winter when the nor'westers come, the wind direction changes from blowing out of the southeast to blowing out of the northwest. Then is the only time our house is on the *leeside* of the island. Whatever side ain't got a wind blowing in its face is the windless leeside.

Like I said before, the Everglades is a very long, very wide, very shallow river that used to flow in an unbroken sheet from Lake Okeechobee to the Gulf of Mexico. For years they have been building *levees* to either drain it for farming or channel it toward the east coast so that the people living over there (Miami to West Palm Beach) have enough water.

Levees is just long banks of shells and dirt—not as fancy as them dikes they got in Holland, but they do the same thing: keep water from where it ain't wanted and force it to go somewhere it wasn't meant to be. Deep water canals run right alongside every levee 'cause that there's where the dirt came from to build it.

Mangrove trees is the most common tree along the coast of south Florida. There are three kinds: the red, the black, and the white. The red mangrove can grow right in salt water and has a tangle of roots called prop roots, which come out of the tree trunk above ground and arch over, growing down through the water and finally into the mud. Mangrove roots is a safe place for baby fish, shrimp, and crab larvae to grow up.

At docks, parking spaces for boats are called *slips*. Each one is separated by a couple of huge posts driven into the muddy bottom. These keep the boats from bumping each other. I never asked the Admiral why they are called slips, and I still ain't of a mind to ask Dad, but they are. My dad has the best one, at the very end, so he can come in the channel and pull straight into his slip.

I don't think I'll ever outgrow fearing storms. On a rainy day when a *squall* suddenly sets all the trees a-blowing like they was gonna pull themselves free of the soil and fly off somewhere, I remember Dad and me that night on Turner River. Instead of being scared, I guess I should try to remember the good that came along near as sudden as them outbursts of wind and rain.

About the Author

GINNY RORBY was born in Washington, D.C., and spent the first twenty years of her life in Winter Park, Florida. She now lives, close to nature, on the northern coast of California, supporting the appetites of five cats (the fourth and fifth appropriately named Spare Cat and Extra Cat), three birds, and a snake named Rosie. Because she does some wildlife rehabilitation, she frequently has an assortment of critters staying with her (past residents have included a bat, a hummingbird, a raven, a turkey, and numerous baby birds.)

She writes, by hand, under a plum tree on a deck overlooking a creek, facing a redwood forest (with at least one cat in her lap). She had been working as a flight attendant for fifteen years when she wrote an editorial about an abandoned dog and sent it to a local newspaper. An editor at the newspaper encouraged her to continue writing. Ginny has since received her MFA in creative writing. She was still flying when she wrote *Dolphin Sky,* so most of it was written while she was standing up in the lower galley of a DC-10 airplane.

This is her first novel.